I0614542

Beyond The Pathway
A Quabbin Quills Anthology

Perpetual Imagination
Boston • Northampton • New York

881 Main St #10
Fitchburg, MA 01420

info@perpetualimagination.com
www.PerpetualImagination.com

info@quabbinquills.org
www.QuabbinQuills.org

Production Copyright © 2021
Quabbin Quills and Perpetual Imagination

Manufactured in The United States of America.

1 2 3 4 5 6 7 8 9 10

First Edition

ISBN-13: 978-1-7352576-1-7

Library of Congress Control Number in process for this title.

Table of Contents

Pathways of Adventure   **103**

Travel, Local, and Nature Writing

Pathways of the Soul   147

Memoir, Grief, and Loss Writing

Pathways of Imagination   **183**

Sci fi, Fantasy, and Paranormal Writing

DEDICATION

This anthology is dedicated to Miryam Ehrlich Williamson, whose tireless efforts of editing the first volume of Quabbin Quills assured the dynamic continuance of this fourth volume. We are heartily grateful for her writing support and respectful editorial guidance.

Miryam has been a freelance writer since 1983, authoring numerous articles and short stories. She wrote over 10 books ranging from her own poetry, true crime, and how to manage various health conditions including *Fibromyalgia: A Comprehensive Approach* and *The Fibromyalgia Relief Book*. She has received acclaim and awards for her work. She has also served as the president of The National Writers' Union.

Communication is central to her expression of life. For ten years, she participated in the Women in Black Peace Vigil in Orange, Massachusetts. Also, she and her late husband, Ed Hawes, initiated and developed the listserve for Warwick, the Warwick-L, so that neighbors could share ideas, needs, concerns, and items of interest. This benefit to the townsfolk continues to the present.

Miryam, longtime resident of Warwick, Massachusetts, now resides at Charlene Manor in Greenfield.

A NOTE FROM THE PRESIDENT

This marks our fourth anthology and we are immensely proud of the work that went into creating this. At first, we had to strategize how best to overcome the hurdles that the global pandemic put before us. The result was a change in the way we accepted our submissions because we could no longer meet in-person with Quabbin area writers to workshop pieces specifically designed for our anthologies. Thanks to technology and Google Docs, our board of editors met to discuss guidelines and worked hard to become writing coaches who could not only critique but inspire improvement in each work. As such, the in-person workshop was replaced by a running commentary viewable by a submission coordinator, an editor, and the author of the piece. With this system in place, no piece was rejected and it all resulted in some very amazing stories and ideas as you will see in the pages ahead.

Meanwhile, our scholarship winners were selected on merit, and these budding and talented writers were quick and eager to accept suggestions that would make their pieces shine more than what stellar work they had already given us. Our scholarship mission has always been a big part of our organization. At the time of this writing, we have awarded six scholarship prizes and we are fortunate enough to have our previous winners publishing new works in this anthology.

As you wander through the pages of this book, take joy in knowing that each piece is unique in the way it provides, not just for the reader but also for the author, some insight and meaning into our everyday lives. Every story is part of a writer's journey and you hold in your hand a first class ticket to extraordinary rides over reservoirs, mountains, and through valleys as you look beyond this path for inspiration for your own grand or relaxing adventure.

Keep on writing on,

Steve Piscitello
President of Quabbin Quills, 2021

SCHOLARSHIP WINNERS 2021

As a previous scholarship winner, I am so pleased to announce the winners of this year's Quabbin Quills writing scholarship: Katelyn Stolberg, Jillian Mawaka, and Violet Masterson. On behalf of the editorial board and all of our readers, I would like to congratulate you on your hard work, commitment to writing, and luminous, captivating poetry and prose. These young authors' pieces are by turns deeply personal, emotionally charged, and introspective, and we are delighted to have them as part of our anthology.

We have selected our talented winners based on the literary merit of their pieces, and in addition to publishing their pieces will be awarding them cash prizes to aid schooling expenses. Education is expensive, and we at Quabbin Quills want you to know that we support the pursuit of higher education.

To our scholarship winners and contributors, congratulations. You should be proud of what you have accomplished. To our readers, I hope you enjoy our scholarship winners' pieces. All three show promise in the literary arts, and we hope that they, like all of our contributors, will continue writing and developing as authors. Now settle in and prepare to be delighted by the scope and power of our local writers. Happy reading!

Cecilia Januszewski

2020 scholarship recipient
Editorial Board Member

PAUSE

Katelyn Stolberg

... --- ...

Studying for assessment

Assessment for potential

Potential for scientist

... --- ...

Salary not volunteer

Complaisant not ambitious

Performance not intellect

.--. .- ..- ... .

What am I doing?

Am I trapped?

Wasn't this path always 'my choice'?

.-- .- ..- ... .

A dirt path,

      trees engulfing both sides.

A small rock,

     the perfect shape for an afternoon of contemplation.

Ants crawling in uniformity with no one leading the other.

     Social complexity and collective intelligence guided by
evolution.

     Ecological wonder and intricacies within a few square feet of
earth.

.--. .- ..- ... .

I sit on this rock.

     I wonder about the world around me.

I want to know the 'simple' life of an ant,

     without becoming one myself.

I am a scientist.

     I do have potential.

I care to study all life

     regardless of salary

with ambitious intellect.

     I am a scientist.

BIRD LADY

Jillian Mawaka

I once met two homeless men on the streets of Northampton who took a beat-up guitar, an upside-down bucket for percussion, and performed a song that they made up for me on the spot.

It happened as I roamed the streets looking for a crystal shop I had driven 30 minutes to find. Two men stopped me to advise me that my overall strap was falling from my shoulder. I already knew the one strap had a faulty clasp, so I politely informed them that I was aware of this wardrobe malfunction. I actually quite liked the aesthetic that the drooping strap gave my olive green one-piece. Yet, I did as a typical chronic people-pleaser does: fixed it immediately.

This seemed to upset one of the men; he proceeded to sit down on the sidewalk before pulling out an old, battered guitar. The other man, who produced a bucket and two tree branches from behind a flower bed, asked if I wanted to be "serenaded."

Now, as a shy, quiet girl from the small rural town of Wilbraham, I would never expect myself to agree to be put on the spot like this. Especially not by two complete strangers who wanted to sing to me on the street. I opened my mouth, ready to oppose, but the only words that tumbled from my lips were:

"Yes, of course! Give me the best you've got!" I was shocked by the fully confident sound of my own voice.

The man tuned his guitar effortlessly and proceeded to recite a song about random nonsense. He sang that I was a witch, or perhaps a magician, or finally, the exotic "bird lady." As the percussionist delivered his "famous" drum solo, I found myself cheering for them as if I was at a concert. Onlookers passed by, clearly confused by the sight unveiling before them, but I just stood there and clapped.

For once in my life, I didn't care what other people were thinking about me; I was fully immersed in this fantastical backstory that this stranger was assigning me after only having known me for a few minutes.

When the "instruments" ceased, I placed three dollars in their open guitar case and thanked them tremendously for their melody.

As I turned to walk away, I heard the guitarist call out to me once more.

"Hey, put your strap back down if that's how you like it!"

I did, and he smiled at me widely.

"Much better!"

I bought my crystals, stopped in a few more forgettable shops, and set off back on the highway with their song on my mind. I wish I had asked for their names, or that they had asked for mine. Yet, I believe they didn't need to know my name to see that I am unsure of who I am. Their song, albeit absurd, resonated with my feelings of uneasiness over my future. I don't know if I am a witch, a magician, a bird lady, or any of these marvelous characters. However, I now strive to take every chance given, allowing each moment to shape me into whatever wondrous individual I am destined to become.

LOVE, CHECK

Violet Masterson

A voice rings in my head, consumes my thoughts, and pulls me into dark water. *Jump in. Go for a swim,* it tells me. I shift in my bed, writhing at the burning thoughts. I cover my eyes with a pillow, trying to block everything out, but all I feel is the darkness rising higher and higher and higher.

My alarm blares, pulling me back to reality. I rub my eyes, dragging myself out of bed. With all the work I have to do, there's no way I can miss school. But how can I spend my day acting as if my head isn't burning with irrational thoughts? *If you don't go to school, you'll fail all your classes and never go anywhere in life. Is that what you want?*

In the bathroom, I turn on the faucet and let the cool water run over my palms. Closing my eyes, I try to ground myself and block out all the bad feelings. *You're such a disaster,* the voice whispers, causing me to flinch. I look in the mirror: my hair is knotted, my undereyes are three shades darker than usual, my lips are dried and cracked, and my eyes are an awful pink. *How are you going to fix all that? Seems like a heavy task.* I sit on the toilet, pressing the heels of my hand into my eyes. *Stop it. Stop it. Stop it!* I force the critical thoughts out of my mind, trying to feel better.

"Jane? You better hurry up or you're going to be late for school," my mom says through the door.

"Mom, I can't go to school today. I really don't feel good," the swelling of the voice forces me to reply.

"Are you okay, sweetie?"

"Yeah, I think I just have a stomach bug or something."

"Okay, well I'll call the school. Go back to bed and get some sleep."

I sigh, relieved. *Dodged that bullet. Now, what terrible things could happen while you're home?*

***

My phone buzzes loudly. I read the wall of texts:

Hope you're feeling better!
I online ordered some ginger ale and antacids from the store for you.
I can get it later, but if you're up to it, you can pick it up.
Just go to customer service and ask for 'mobile order for Emily.'
Love you!
-Mom

I roll over in my bed, ignoring the text. *Nothing* could be worse than going to the store right now, but I could really use some fresh air … *But*—the voice begins. *But nothing,* I spit at it. I need to get out of the house, if only for a minute.

I pull on clean clothes, brush my hair, brush my teeth, and grab my keys. I step outside, my lungs sting, and my whole body freezes. I breathe in more, my body restarting. As my nose begins to go numb, I take to my car and drive down the road.

At the store, I sit in the parking lot for a while. I reread the text from my mom, making sure I know exactly what to do. *Mobile order for Emily. Mobile order for Emily. Mobile order for Emily,* I repeat, drilling it into my brain. *Mobile order for Emily. Mobile order for Emily.* Walking into the store, I hesitantly go to the customer service counter.

"Hello, how can I help you today?"

"H- Hi. I'm um … here f-for a mobile order for Emily, please."

"No, problem. Let me just grab it."

My breath is caught, and I stand there for a few seconds. Before I can stop it, the voice creeps in again. *He thinks you're pathetic. You can't even ask for a simple order without turning into a mess.*

"Here you go, ma'am," the man hands me a small bag and signals the next customer forward.

"Thank you," I rush out of the way and out the front doors. January coolness on my skin seems to kill whatever the voice has to say.

"Check?"

I whip my head around, Naya Wyley is pushing carts. I've never seen her outside of chemistry or talked to her about anything other than formulas and equations.

"Oh, hey, Naya."

"What're you doing here? Shouldn't you be at school? I've never known you to miss a day," she walks towards me, abandoning her carts.

"Sick day. I'm just picking up some stuff. Shouldn't *you* be in school?"

"Nah, I couldn't find anyone to cover my shift, and I really can't lose this job. I was just planning on copying notes and homework tomorrow. But since you're out, I guess I'm screwed for chemistry," she laughs, grabbing my bag and poking through it. "Ginger Ale and tums … rough night, Check?"

"Rough morning, really …" my cheeks burn scarlet.

"You don't look sick … but you do look *exhausted.*"

"Well, that's always a side effect …"

"Hey, did you know I have a third eye?" Naya points between her eyebrows, a smile spreading across her face. "Yeah, it usually sees through people's bullshit."

"I- I don't know what you're talking about."

"What I mean is, I know you're not sick. So, what's really wrong?"

"Nothing. I just don't feel well."

"And ginger ale is going to fix that?"

"I just … why do you even care?"

My face is even hotter now.

"No need to get defensive, Check. I'm just looking out for you. I see those spacey looks you get in chemistry."

"Wha-what looks?"

People notice you. They see you and judge you and think you're crazy, the voice in my head says.

"Sort of like the look you have on your face now. Your face goes bright red, you stop talking, you refuse to make eye contact with anyone, and nothing you say seems genuine anymore."

"I-I—"

"Listen, whatever you're feeling, Ginger Ale isn't gonna fix it. You need to do something, *get out* for a minute. Did you drive here?"

"Yeah, I did."

"Great. Give me your keys."

"What? Why?"

"You'll see," Naya smiles.

Don't do it. Who knows what she has planned.

Naya holds out a long, olive hand, waiting for my keys. I don't want to go with her, but when I try to think of why, the only reasons I have are given to me by the wretched, little voice. So, when she starts to pull back her hand, I grab it and shove my keys into her palm.

"So, where are we going?"

"That's my girl," she smiles even bigger than before.

***

"Wait, aren't you supposed to be ... well ... doing your job?" I ask, buckling myself into the passenger seat of my car.

"Yeah, well, this is more important."

"But won't you get fired?"

"Check, that's not important right now. What's important is helping you get over whatever 'bug' you have."

She's gonna get fired because of you. Then she'll hate you, never talk to you again, and everything will be terrible. Guilt rises in me; I try to stifle it, hoping Naya won't notice, but it doesn't work.

"Hey," she says, softer than ever before. She grabs my hand and looks at me. "I fucking hate this job. I'm okay leaving it for one afternoon."

"Then why didn't you go to school?"

"Choosing between that hell hole and this one wasn't that hard. At least here I don't have to do trigonometry or run laps around a smelly, old gym. You ready?"

Naya, for whatever reason, has an effect on me that I can't explain. Her enticing smile and soothing words seem to enchant me. I'm somehow excited and ready for whatever she has planned.

"Yeah, I'm ready."

Naya smiles and races out of the parking lot. I grab onto the bar above my head, staring at her with my mouth agape. *She's going to kill us. Your mom will find out you died with a lunatic driving your car.*

"Oh, live a little, Check!"

Roads that I usually soak in speed by in a blur. Naya streaks past cars, weaves in and out of lanes, races people who are completely unaware, and blares the music. She switches the station to some loud one I don't recognize and sings along with the incomprehensible lyrics. I can't help but notice how Naya sings; despite her hard exterior, and the volume at which she plays her music, her voice is euphonious.

"What?" she asks.

"What?"

"You're staring at me."

"Oh, it's just that your voice is really pretty … Do you sing?"

"Not outside of my shower or my car. And now your car, I guess."

"Well you should. You sound really nice."

"It's not really my vibe, singing all pretty."

"I think it suits you."

Naya smiles at me again, but a softer smile than she's shown before. She faces the road again, hums along with the song, and taps her finger to the beat. For the first time, I really look at her. Her hair is ebony, but the ends are a bright blue; her dark eyeliner is smudged, dragged all around her eyelid and waterline; her nose is long and slim, shining with a silver hoop; she wears a leather jacket, layers of long sleeves, ripped jeans, and black boots; she has a million different piercings: different size hoops, different color gems, and different shapes adorn her ears, shining behind her hair. Her fingers are beringed, she wears necklaces upon necklaces, and her nails are a chipped maroon. It seems like she let her guard down, because for the first time since I've known her, she looks ... soft.

Naya's driving slows down as we reach, what I assume, is our destination.

"Where are we?"

"My dad's house. I'll be right back," Naya steps out of the car, runs along a shoveled path, and emerges a few minutes later with two sleds.

"What are those for?"

"Surfing. What do you think they're for? We're going sledding!"

"I ... Why?"

"Because sledding is fun, and you need a little fun in your life," she shrugs, throwing the sleds in my back seat.

"You don't know my life! I do fun things!"

"Oh yeah, like what? Drink tea and read Jane Austen?" Naya snorts.

"What's wrong with Jane Austen?"

"Oh my God! I was joking, but now we really need to have some fun. And there's nothing wrong with Jane Austen," Naya smiles and speeds down the road.

***

The snow is just beginning to fall as Naya sets down her sled. She sits, excitement spreading across her face. Handing me a small, circular sled, she motions for me to join her. I sit on it, fear heating up my frozen skin. *You're going to break your arm. Or your neck.*

"Be honest, Check, when was the last time you went sledding?"

"Never," I look down the steep hill, the ice gleaming greatly.

"How have you never been sledding?"

"I was always too scared as a kid! I didn't want to break an arm, and I don't want to break one today."

"Check, sledding is targeted for children, and as two seventeen year olds, I'm sure we'll be fine. Just take my hand, hold that strap, and get ready."

Naya's icy hand grabs my hot one. Nerves fill my whole body, but also excitement. I squeeze her hand tightly as she counts "ONE, TWO, THREE, GO!" and pushes us down the hill.

We race down, sliding across the slick snow. Flakes fly into my eyes, freezing my face and blinding me. The wind whips through my hair, a chill bites at my ears and nose. Suddenly, the sleds fly over a jump, sending us into the air. *You're going to crash and break something, then you'll really be sorry.* We soar for a moment—a glorious moment—and hit the ground with a painful *thud.* Naya's hand slips from mine as she falls out of her sled and rolls across the frozen ground.

"Naya!"

She's injured, or dead, because of you. She wouldn't be here if she didn't pity you so much. If she's hurt, it's all on you.

I run towards her, slipping and sliding. I land next to her and find her rolling around, laughing.

"That was incredible! Come on, let's go again," she jumps up, grabs my hand, and pulls me back up the hill.

"I thought you died!"

"Check, I promise you, neither of us are going to die sledding. It just won't happen. Now, let's go again."

This time, Naya makes me go down alone. The fear recedes, joy taking its place. We race back and go down on a sled together, holding onto each other for dear life; we race on our separate sleds; we go over all the jumps, and then make new jumps when we decide they're not high enough. The rest of the park begins to fill as the elementary kids are let out for the day, and soon enough, the hill is full.

"Okay, do you want to try something else?" Naya asks me, sitting on the wet pavement.

"Like what?"

"Ice skating," she looks across the road at the frozen pond.

"We don't have skates, and besides, there's no way I'm skating on a frozen pond."

"And why is that?"

"It could break! You could fall in and *die!*"

"Okay first of all, this isn't *The Good Son.* Second, the city checks to make sure the ice is thick enough for civilian safety."

"But, but—"

"And, if you did fall in, the water is approximately two feet deep. You'd just be freezing for a couple hours."

Yeah. Freezing, hypothermia, frostbite, death. Sounds fun.

"You go first, then I'll try." I say, steadying my nerves.

"Okay, I'm not afraid," Naya stands up and walks straight onto the ice. She slips, catches herself, and walks further out. "Come on in, the water's fine!" she laughs.

Hesitantly, I walk onto the ice. I step onto it, putting my full weight down, and wait for it to crack. It doesn't.

"See? Perfectly safe," Naya takes my hands and pulls me along, shuffling her feet.

"This isn't so ba—" I begin to say, but I'm cut off when I slip and fall on top of Naya.

You idiot. She's gonna think you're so stupid.

Naya cackles, rubbing her elbow.

"Oh my god, are you okay? I'm so sorry!" Heat creeps into my face.

"I'm okay! I'm okay! Don't worry. Hey, don't worry, Jane," Naya says my name softly—pushing back my hair and tucking it behind my ear.

"You called me Jane."

"That's your name, isn't it?"

"Yeah, but you usually call me Check."

"I think Jane is a pretty name."

"Naya's one, too."

Naya gazes into my eyes for a minute, looking like she's thinking about something really hard. She's about to say something when we're interrupted.

"Hey, you ladies okay?" a man yells.

"All good!" Naya yells to the man, but turns back to me. "Come with me. I wanna take you somewhere."

***

"How much further?" I pant.

"Not much, just come on! It's worth it."

Naya drags me up a small, eroded path, leading to god knows where. *Why would you follow someone you barely know into the woods?* I push the voice away, soaking in the scenery. The snow is falling thicker now, slicking what little of the ground we have to walk on. The forest is dense with trees; the trunks are a pale brown, and the bare tops blend into the white sky.

"Here."

We turn up a bend and land on a flat stretch of snow-covered ground. At the very front is a small, wooden bench, looking over the entire city. As the sun begins to make it's early descent, the city is illuminated by a warm, orange haze. Bright lights are turned on, spreading stars across the city. There's no noise but faint laughter of families at the park.

"It's ... beautiful."

"Isn't it? I come here a lot, whenever I need to think," Naya takes my hand again and leads me to the bench. Sitting us down, she wraps an arm around me.

Naya and I sit for a while, enjoying the view. Her warm arm is wrapped around my shoulders, pressing me close to her. My cheeks grow warm, but not out of embarrassment or as a result of the little voice. Neither of us talk for a while, but just enjoy each other's company. Suddenly, Naya shifts, her face serious.

"I came here everyday after my mom kicked me out. When I was sixteen, I lived with her. Everything was fine until she read my journal one day and found out ... and found out I was—well, am—a lesbian. She was furious. She said she didn't want to live with someone 'like me.' She made me leave, and I had nowhere to go. No family would take me in, and my dad hadn't moved here yet. So for a while, I stayed here. This is where I'd think. I'd sit for hours, just trying to figure out what to do. Eventually, I reached out to an older friend of mine, and she offered to let me stay with her. I got a job, and I've been living there ever since."

"Naya, I'm so—"

"It's okay. You don't need to be sorry. I'm happier now than I ever was when I lived with my mom. When I was with her, a little voice constantly rang in my head. It would just tell me how *worthless* I was, and I believed it. For a while, I thought all the nasty things my mom—and that voice—said were true. But eventually I realized how wrong they were. I'm proud of who I am, and I'll never change that for anybody. Not even my own mother."

My face burns greatly, deepening in color. Naya, this girl who's so confident, strong, and who I've been bewildered by all day, has that little voice in her head too. *So you both are crazy,* the voice tries to convince me.

"That voice you're talking about … how did you stop it?"

"I didn't. It can't be stopped, but it can be quieted. It used to scream at me so loudly everyday, but now it just whispers occasionally," Naya looks at me and wipes a hot tear from my cheek. "All I had to do was learn how to love myself, and talk to someone—let them help me through it. You can quiet that voice, I know you can. You deserve to walk around like the amazing girl you are."

I close my eyes and drink in all she's saying, more tears steam on my cold cheeks. Naya wipes them away and pulls me closer.

"Thank you, Naya. For everything today."

***

Naya and I sit in the quiet for a long time, watching the sun sink behind the city. Orange and yellow are smeared across the sky, fading into the night. The street lights shine brighter now and stars dance across the horizon. Darkness begins to fill the sky, taking over all that the sun used to hold. The air grows colder, freezing every bit of us. Large snowflakes slowly drift from the sky, melting on our cheeks and in our hair.

"As much as I don't want to, we should probably go. You know, before we freeze to death," Naya says.

I nod, and we stand up. She holds my hand, steadying me. We walk through the long stretch of snow, but after a few steps, we slip. *Idiot! Idiot! Idiot!* I knock Naya down, landing on top of her, and we burst into laughter.

"Are you okay?" I ask through my laughing, as I push hair out of her eyes.

"Yeah. I'm okay, Jane."

"You called me Jane again."

"Yeah … It's a pretty name. I like Jane."

"Naya is a pretty name, too. I like Naya."

She tucks my hair behind my ear and looks deep into my eyes. *Don't do it. She'll think you're a creep and never talk to you ever again,* the voice rattles in my head. But before I can doubt myself any more, I lean down and kiss her. Naya's top lip meets my bottom one, her hand finds my cheek, and mine finds her hair. When our cold lips meet, they warm instantly. That warmth spreads all through me, down to my fingertips and toes. My heart leaps, and my stomach does backflips. Pure joy takes over me, and once again, I'm completely enchanted by her. We stay there for a moment, soaking it all in.

"That was bold, Jane. I liked it."

"Yeah, well … I've decided I want to have a little fun in my life."

"That's my girl," Naya smiles.

PATHWAYS OF REFLECTION

Memoir, Life, and Inspirational Writing

DIVINE INTERVENTION

Sharon Ann Harmon

"I can't believe we found this place!" I said to my husband. It was May 2020 of COVID-19, and we had been taking hikes to places we had never been. We were retired and trying to stay healthy. For years, we had passed this river that looked like a trail ran alongside it on the far bank.

At last, I convinced my husband that we should check it out. We took the 25-minute ride from our house. A huge red and white covered bridge traversed the river; we drove through it and parked. It was indeed an old railway trail. We walked and walked, enjoying the river and the solitude of the woods all alone.

At last, we saw an old bridge span in ruin halfway across the river. When we got to where it was, we found a heap of an old demolished brick factory. My heart leapt when I saw the discarded bricks.

I owned only one like it. It was a gift from my son-in-law, a building contractor. He had found it on a job while remodeling an old house. It now sat in my garden with roses spilling over it.

The word on it said *PRAY*.

We found three good intact ones and lugged them another mile back to the car. I felt like I was walking with weights, but I didn't care. I had plans for them.

When we arrived home, we chipped old mortar off the bricks. Then we poured lime cleaner on them and scrubbed them with a brush.

We put the bricks in bags and drove around, leaving them on doorsteps of loved ones as a surprise with a little note. "Hope you can find a place for this in your garden," it simply stated.

In a time of loneliness due to the pandemic, everyone who received one was overwhelmed with love and renewed hope from our little gift.

MORNING OF THE NEW

John Grey

Sun's the perfect auditor.

Turns up an insect or two

as well as the face

buoyant between dreams and sleep.

Shadows vanish

at the onset of replenishing yawns.

Decorous bedroom,

the poetry of dreams

is reduced to an invigorating couplet.

Are you awake?

It's too early for profundity.

I'll take delight.

Your eyes open,

much enlarged

from what I remember.

Breath may have some

catching up to do

but, other than that,

perfect.

Days always should begin

with vicissitude,

the good fortune

of ordinary lives.

Something fabulously intrinsic

so that, even if it's not morning,

it really is.

Everything new begins now.

Here's the promise

of what's yet unlived.

Any regrets?

No need to answer.

Second-thoughts are blasphemy

right about now.

BEACH PLUM PATH

Lauren Milka

As the sun peeked over the horizon, the tide would reveal different objects on the shore that had traveled through the sea many nights before: colorful shells in all shapes and sizes, tangled seaweed, upturned crabs, and open-mouthed mollusks that had met their fate by seagulls, and the occasional driftwood. There was always something new to discover and collect.

The thick, salty scent of the ocean twisted its way through her open bedroom window, tangling itself with the smells of freshly brewed coffee and warm muffins just out of the oven from the bakery down the road. It was the same every morning, every summer, for as long as she could remember.

The little girl sprang out of bed and bounded down the stairs to the kitchen, greeting her grandmother and parents and immediately begging them to go to the beach. Shortly after breakfast, she led the family down the sandy path in the backyard, running ahead of them—passing by the beach plum bushes and bayberry shrubs—until she could see the swaying strands of eelgrass ahead. She stopped just at the edge of the path's end, breathing in the salty air until her lungs were full and exhaling with a smile.

As a child, her favorite things to collect were seashells of every size and color to line up along the windowsill in her bedroom. Inevitably, they would be forgotten at the end of the summer in the hustle and bustle of packing up to return to the city. Her grandmother would scoop them up and add them to a jar of seashells from summers past that she kept on top of her bookcase. As she grew older, her grandmother taught her how to turn these seashells into jewelry and pieces of art, and even painted Christmas ornaments.

Summers passed, but the tide still produced its offerings to the waiting shore as promised each day. The winding, sandy path to the ocean had many pairs of bare and sandaled feet run along it and out towards the beach.

Her most treasured item she found hid beneath a pile of seaweed during the summer she turned sixteen. One bright sunny morning, she found a small piece of light blue sea glass, the color of the Mediterranean. She pocketed the piece in her shorts, and upon returning to the house, showed her grandmother her discovery. It was almost identical to the light blue sea glass tied in the delicately twisted wire bracelet the grandmother wore on her wrist. That afternoon, her grandmother had left a gift for her on the kitchen table—a wire bracelet of her own with the blue sea glass at the center.

So many years later, the sun winked momentarily from behind the fluffy cumulus clouds, catching its rays on the old piece of sea glass in her bracelet. The weathered beach house had been through four generations, with the fifth arriving soon. The girl, now a grandmother herself, stood at the kitchen sink, sipping her coffee and gazing out the window over the yard to the sliver of sand she could see in her mind's eye.

Excerpts From
CLOSE ENOUGH TO PERFECT

Christine Noyes

It rained the day he died. Not the battering drops of a magnificently fierce midsummer thunderstorm but the gentle mist of an unseasonably tepid January predawn in New England. It was two in the morning on Saturday as Al and I gathered the final few bathroom items to cram into our oversized, airline-approved carry-on bags. One cup of coffee would have to suffice, as we had a ninety-minute drive to the airport and, at our age, bathroom stops became more pressing and plentiful on their own. Additional stimulants could prove problematic.

Huh! The things we worry about when we don't know that our lives will soon change forever.

The sun still slept as we loaded the car, remarkably on schedule, to leave for Las Vegas. Al struggled with his breathing, having fallen victim to the cold I had the previous week. Seemingly, he could not inhale enough air to satisfy his need, his cadenced effort going unrewarded.

Early winter mornings in Massachusetts can be hazardous, no matter what the current weather produced. Even when the temperatures hover above freezing, roads can take on a shine, either innocently wet from dew or perilously dangerous from dreaded black ice. It had been unusually warm as we made our way along Millers River towards Route 91, and as the temperature rose, so rose the fog. Al was behind the wheel of our white Dodge Journey meandering along the winding two-lane road—twenty miles an hour over the speed limit.

I suppose it should have occurred to me earlier, but it was not until we reached the first curve, contacted black ice, and glided off the road towards a six-foot ditch did I consider maybe I should be behind the wheel. The rear tires struggled to keep hold of the frozen shoulder as Al instinctively spun the wheel into an overexaggerated left-hand turn and then a course-correcting right. As he regained control, I heard myself cursing, adamantly announcing my displeasure with his driving. I told him to pull over at the convenience store just ahead. I would drive. He didn't argue. He didn't dispute. That's when it sunk in how horrible he must have felt.

And then the first twinges of guilt set in.

I learned, early on, how to deal with guilt. How to turn it off, pack it away, and on occasion, ignore it. I've also learned that guilt and regret frequently go hand in hand. But regrets are tricky, because we usually think of them out of context based on retrospective analysis, and then know after the fact what we didn't know before. Regrets tend to linger like unwelcome fumes from a frightened skunk. But how potent and influential regrets can be, and how difficult to live with the odor.

Guilt, however, is a by-product of a conscious decision, which makes it powerful, predominant, and precarious … like nearly ending up in a ditch because you should have made the decision to drive in the first place.

We drove in silence. Al's struggle for breath amplified.

* * *

When I was twenty-six and working as a cook at the Mountain Barn Restaurant, my coworker Paul badgered me to join the tenpin bowling team he and others had formed. The league had just begun, and one of the team members backed out at the last minute. They needed a fourth person to round out the team or they would have to drop out of the league. I refused multiple times, but Paul persisted, and finally, I reluctantly agreed. I hadn't bowled since my childhood Saturday morning candlepin league. I hoped Paul and his friends would need a fill-in only for the first week until they got a permanent fourth member.

Fate had a different plan.

Our opponents arrived with gear bags in hand, freshly laundered shirts with team logo and name, and confidence that swelled as they scanned our side of the mint-green bench.

He drew my attention from the moment I saw him.

Not very tall and overweight, he nevertheless carried himself with assurance both authentic and unassuming. As he laced up his bowling shoes, I noticed his hands: working hands, not chafed or dry, but strong and reliable. There's something about a man's hands that I find telling and intriguing.

He reached into his bag, retrieved a blue-marbled, custom-fit bowling ball, and placed it on the ball-return rack. As he walked back to the bench, I could read his name stitched on the left front of his shirt above the pocket—Al. And as destiny would have it, I would bowl directly against him.

Before arriving to meet my other teammates, I had resigned myself to the likelihood that I would make a fool of myself, and they would happily replace me the following week. And even though I am a very competitive person, I felt fine with that—until I saw Al.

I hadn't practiced, I sported well-worn rented bowling shoes, and I had chosen a ten-pound alley-owned ball, the lightest one I could find among the venue's selections. I knew how to bowl, but tenpin bowling posed a distinctly different challenge than using the smaller, lighter candlepin balls I grew up with. Candlepin balls weigh less than three pounds, and you have three chances to knock the pins down instead of two. But the concept was the same. Roll the first ball between the number three and four arrows marked on the lane fifteen feet ahead of the foul line and pray that the ball went straight. If it did, I wouldn't have to worry about slinging the second shot because I'd be celebrating my perfectly thrown strike with my teammates.

He was left-handed. When he released his fifteen-pound ball, it traveled along the left gutter lip for two-thirds of the journey until the violent spin he torqued it with gripped the lane and drove it toward the pins. It fascinated me to watch. I imagined it took considerable strength to hurl.

Our opposing styles showcased the difference between a novice and a practiced participant of the sport. Because it was so obvious, I knew I had nothing to lose. When I have nothing to lose, I can give my very best effort without stressing over the outcome, and I did exactly that. I thoroughly enjoyed the short banter we shared between each frame. I found him smart, funny, clever, and not nearly as competitive as I had imagined.

I don't recall keeping track of the score, but when we finished the first string, as improbable as it sounds, I had beaten him. He would later use the excuse that I had distracted him from the moment he saw me. He was a sweet talker. As we continued with the next two strings, the bowling universe went back on track, and our team got trounced.

The bowling alley had its own full-service bar, so with the business of bowling behind us, my teammates and I went into the bar for a few beers. Hoping to see Al among the patrons, I scanned the crowded room. I felt surprisingly disappointed when I didn't find him there. That was surprising because I wasn't looking for a man in my life. I had long before resigned myself to thinking that I wouldn't succeed at relationships, so I felt no need to pursue one. But I suspected something different this time. I felt drawn to him.

I had nearly finished my first beer when he walked into the bar and skimmed the room. I spied him instantly because I hadn't taken my eyes off the door since we sat down. He spotted me spotting him, walked past the table where his teammates gathered, and took a seat beside me. Eventually, as the room began to empty, we moved up to the bar. Never missing a beat, we talked non-stop—no uncomfortable silence or searching for the right words. We talked about our childhoods, our goals, our work, and for some reason that I can't remember, we went through each other's wallets. It was easy, it was familiar, it was thrilling, it was wonderful. At some point, we realized we were the only two left in the bar besides the incredibly patient bartender, the only one of us who wanted the night to come to an end. So Al and I sat in the parking lot, talking and listening to music until four o'clock in the morning.

Had we met during the era of cell phones and social media the following week might not have been so agonizing. We hadn't exchanged phone numbers, most likely because neither one of us spent any time at home. Because of the lack of contact during that week and my lack of confidence, I talked myself into thinking I had imagined how well we hit it off. I recall a telephone conversation with my mother as I recounted the night's interactions and told her that I had most likely misconstrued the entire evening, that he probably hadn't thought about me at all.

Unlike the first week, my wish of a one-week engagement long forgotten, I looked forward to the arrival of the second bowling night. I got to the alley a bit early. A quick search revealed that Al hadn't arrived, so I checked the schedule on the board to see the lane assigned to my team that night. I also checked to see Al's lane. His team would bowl at the opposite end of the building, too far away for a chance run-in.

As those thoughts swirled in my head, I noticed Jane, one of Al's teammates, heading toward me. Except for the usual niceties, I hadn't really spoken to her the week before, but she greeted me like an old friend and told me that Al was at night school and would show up later that evening. She said she had strict orders not to let me leave until he got there. I feigned indifference, but all the while, my insides did a little jig. He had thought about me after all.

I had never let myself get close to anyone or let them see me—the real me—until that day in October of 1987 when I went bowling. In my few previous relationships, I found myself unable to participate actively, too unsure of myself to interject my own thoughts or emotions. Yet, on that first night with Al, I told him things I had never told anyone, intensely personal and private things.

Some might call it love at first sight, although I think that's a little melodramatic. However, we experienced something special. Something I couldn't quite explain happened the night we met. It felt as if we had known each other forever, yet I had never laid eyes on him. I felt comfortable with him from the start, yet I had never felt comfortable with any man. The feeling I had—and still have—is that we had done it all before.

* * *

Once in his seat, Al's wheezy and labored breathing seemed to improve. I could tell passengers filled up seats around us, but it didn't stop me from falling into a state between consciousness and sleep. I'm pretty sure Al did the same.

We were in the air; I vaguely remembered the takeoff process. I heard Al's voice break through my sleepy fog. He needed to use the restroom. Slightly annoyed and without uttering a word, I got up and moved into the aisle to let him out. He walked to the front of the airplane, through first class, and entered the lavatory. I reasoned that I would have to wait for him to come back before I could sleep again. My heavy lids closed.

I felt a tap on my shoulder. I opened my weary eyes to see the airline attendant leaning over me.

"Is that your husband in the restroom?" she asked.

I looked to my left, saw the empty seat, and replied, "Yes."

She told me she had knocked on the bathroom door and hadn't gotten an answer.

I fought through my sleepy haze of a brain and remembered he had been gone a long time, and I had thought he must have been having trouble negotiating the small room. How long had I been sleeping?

"He's not feeling well," I explained.

She asked if I would check on him. We walked to the front of the airplane to the restroom near the galley and cockpit door. She reached to the top of the door, flipped a lever or switch that only airline personnel would know, and the door swung open towards her to give me a little privacy.

He fell asleep, I thought. He could sleep very soundly when he's this tired.

I spoke his name . . . nothing. I spoke it again a little louder.

I lightly slapped his cheek, then a little harder.

He felt cold.

"He's not responding," I heard myself say.

I began to feel ethereal as if constructed of vapors, not of this world but watching as the world unfolded before my eyes. What seemed like minutes must have passed in seconds as time became obsolete. I watched as the woman performed CPR on my husband. The only words I remember her saying? "I don't have a pulse" and "We have to get him out of here."

It felt surreal. I couldn't fully process the contents of my own thoughts, fragments of a broken mirror that didn't fit together properly as they floated in the mist of my consciousness.

For the first time since I felt that tap of guilt, the words, *what happens if* . . . crept into my head and *what if I had . . . regret.*

Al died on that plane, surrounded by strangers heroically trying to save his life.

When I began writing my memoir, I did it just for me. I felt it was my way of ejecting the pain from my heart. But, as with most therapeutic activities, the process taught me I needn't eject the pain. I should embrace it, celebrate it. For if I didn't have the pain, I didn't have the love.

I never know what sight, sound, or smell will trigger my emotions. Grief mostly hits me without warning like the pop of a water bottle, as if to remind me that things can change in an instant.

Not long after he died, I drove Al's Dodge Journey along a back road in our hometown when I heard the familiar pop, the sound you get when you stick the tip of your index finger inside your mouth and pluck the cheek.

I instantly began to cry and laugh at the same time.

Al kept a partially full plastic water bottle in the passenger seat cup holder. In colder months, the bottle collapsed. With the car heat on, the bottle warmed up to expand the plastic, causing it to make that popping sound.

After the sound startled me several times, I asked Al why he didn't throw the plastic bottle away. He explained that he had become accustomed to using it as a time reference when he drove to work, since it popped at almost the same spot in his travel every day. He found it somehow reassuring.

And then, so did I.

POEMS

Kathy Chencharik

PANDEMIC 2020

Like the Spanish Flu of 2018
This pandemic will someday be gone
Along with those we've loved and lost
As we struggle to carry on.

Beyond the pathway, there is a light
A light at the end of the tunnel
COVID-19 will fade like the winds
Ending a tornado's funnel.

When that day comes, we will celebrate
As we gather together at last
Without fear of infecting each other
With hope that pandemics remain in the past.

COVID-19

I'll live in a bubble
And keep out of trouble
To avoid catching COVID-19.

I will stick to the task
And keep wearing a mask
Until I get the Covid vaccine!

WAITING TO GO ON

Virginia Davis

Summer had already put its spin on the city. Late in May, the sun shined higher and warmer on my face. I put on my pashmina—the color of dusted beach roses, the last gift you ever bought me—and walked the five city blocks to Karlo's for coffee. When Henry Perkins called the Saturday before Memorial Day and asked if he should open the house, I said 'yes' without thinking it through, because that is what we always said.

Two weeks later, programmed by habit, I load the car with shorts, tee shirts, and neglected books waiting to be read. These were the same books that had been stacked neatly on the floor at the end of our bed, wearing a winter's coat of dust. I drive into Maine. The slogan on the highway sign boasts that it's *The Way Life Should Be,* and I find myself briefly wondering if this is so. As I make a right onto Ridgeway, I soon pull into the driveway of our beach house. Inside, I put a pot of water on for tea. As boiling water fizzles over ashy flakes of Earl Grey, I realize that I am waiting for you to bring in our things.

A summer moon is quick to pick up the slack when the sun surrenders. The temperature drops as I walk across the lawn; my bare feet dampened by dewy grass as a chill grazes my shoulders. I open the trunk and find the bag that contains my pajamas and leave everything else in the car.

***

The next day, I wake up late and hungry. I buy take-out at The Fisherman's Fry, then drive north by the access road to the marina, turn around in a nearby driveway clearly marked not to do so, and then circle back. This time, I force myself to drive in, eat my clam strips and French fries directly from the red and white striped paper cartons, and sit in the marina's parking lot. Feeling five pounds heavier, I wipe grease from my chin and dab at a spot between my legs where a bit of tartar sauce has splotched the car's seat cover.

Through the windshield, I watch as the owners, Toola and Ajay, roll and adjust amber bamboo blinds and light tiny oil lanterns at each table in The Anchored-Inn's dining room. I carefully wipe my mouth and reapply a lip balm that leaves no color but smells like coconut sunblock. I check myself in the rear view window and take a deep breath. I step outside.

***

The Anchored-Inn Bar and Grille has reopened for another season. In the graveled parking lot, my pace allows me enough time to notice that they haven't repaired the crack in the porthole window over the front door. The letter "O" is also still missing from the blue and green Open for Business sign tacked to the decaying shingles.

The telephone pole is still there, two-thirds of it anyway—damaged and strapped to a new pole for support. I suppose the town will fully replace it as soon as they can. Although with every passing week, I am inclined to believe that it serves as a totem reminder, as if I could forget. The skid marks in the gravel are still present too, preserved by winter frost. But over time they will shift and mellow into obscurity.

***

Early June heat shocks my skin. I feel your whisper, soft and warm in my ear, urging me to engage the auto-lock on my keychain—an essential habit when living in Andover. However, it is one we hardly ever practice here, even in the summer when travelers increase the population ten times over.

Inside, the overhead fans offer relief from the heat. There are only a handful of locals, mostly stern men back from hauling and Tom Currier who is a charter guide. It is early for the happy hour crowd as I move towards our table overlooking the parking lot. My dress catches on the heavily lacquered bench as I slide over to make room for you, although that is something I no longer need to consider. I like to sit where I can see the marina, the sailboats, the lobster boats, and the occasional yacht. Between the two of us, I was always the one who wanted the view of escape.

"Ah, Miss Coombs, good to see you again!" Toola sets a glass of white wine in front of me; the glass wears beads of perspiration like translucent pearls around a sweating neck.

"Some lunch? New menus this year. I leave you one, maybe two. You are waiting, no?"

"Yes, I am waiting," I smile at Toola too widely, uneasily. I don't like to think I lie often enough to be good at it. "But this will do just fine for now. Thank you."

As I lift the glass to my lips, I realize it is the first time in months that I have ordered anything alcoholic in public.

When I searched the SUV for an earring, I found a half-empty bottle of whiskey under the driver's seat. I was going to ask you what this was all about, but I kept putting it off. I feel as if this implicates me somehow.

***

In the parking lot, a family of five struggle out of an older model station wagon with Oklahoma tags. They stretch their legs as the car doors open one by one.

Two boys and a girl appear with a woman and a man. The man lifts his chin, motioning with his head for them to go on ahead while he leans one elbow on top of the car.

The children wear shorts, tee shirts, and dirty white sneakers without socks. The woman is wearing a sundress with red and white polka-dots. She is tall with a cinched waist so tiny she looks like a paper doll. A slight breeze flirts with her skirt and she wraps the hem around her bare legs with one hand while she adjusts a handbag more securely over her shoulder. The man is wearing clothing for a cooler day, trousers with a long-sleeved button up shirt, and a suit jacket with the kind of wrinkles in the back indicative of long travel.

The woman and children stride to the bar and she orders

hamburgers and four lemonades to go. Ajay sets the four lemonades on the counter. The boys each take two and head to an open booth while the girl and the woman look for the washroom. The woman pulls on the little girl's hand and points to the restroom sign on the wall. The girl whispers something in the woman's ear then gives me a doleful glance over her shoulder.

In January, a week after I returned to work, Rosie Esponita, a fifth grader I had in class last year, passed me a sympathy card at lunchtime. Her father, a city planner, died two years ago, overdosing after developing an opiate addiction from painkillers, prescribed for an old ski injury.

"This is from my mom and me," Rosie said, as she placed her little hand over mine which seemed to me a very mature gesture for an eleven-year-old. At the end of a kind condolence, her mother Carmen added at the bottom of the card: *remember that whatever the cause, a loss is still a loss.* I read this over and over and thought this is a woman who knows.

If we had decided to have children, I would not have been left alone. They would have ensured that I engaged in hobbies I had no interest in; invited me to dinner parties to dine with people I didn't know.

When sleep wouldn't come the previous night at the inn, I put the kettle on for tea. Everything felt as if I were living in a sea-shell— walking around glossy pastel insides, the color of a mellow sunset, fearful of the walls breaking by too much buffering of the wind.

***

The two boys sit at a corner booth and carefully pull straws halfway free of their jackets. They blow the covers at each other; paper airplanes flying over their heads. I allow myself a healthy swallow of my drink and think maybe I will order another.

The woman and the little girl return from the restroom. The girl is upset. She stomps one dirty sneaker on the floor and tries to grab her cup of lemonade which one the boys holds high above his head out of her reach. When he tires of teasing, he passes it back to her. She realizes then that the boys have already peeled the paper covering from her straw. She does not want a straw the boys have touched. She starts to cry which makes the boys laugh. The woman goes to the counter for more straws.

I see you are from Oklahoma. Most of our visitors are from Massachusetts or Canada," Ajay says.

He points outside toward their car. I look out the window. The man walks a few yards toward the marina. He crushes his cigarette under his heel and stuffs his hands in the pockets of his pants as he leans on the rail separating the parking lot from the dock.

The woman shakes her head from side to side quickly. She has the kind of hair that wouldn't move in a tornado. Her skin is pale, like she has never experienced a sunny day. There is a small circle of blue like a bruise above one elbow.

"No, I am actually from Maine. Just a couple hours north of

here. Ever hear of Westport? It's near Boothbay; don't feel bad if you haven't, no one has heard of Westport. But you say you live near Boothbay and everyone knows where that is." She speaks quickly and plays with a piece of her hair, twirling it around her fingers.

"Anyway, we're here to visit my family. I haven't seen them since the day I got married—over twelve years ago," she adds triumphantly as if deserving of a prize.

"Where in Oklahoma do you live?" Ajay asks.

"We live in Goldsby," she tells him. "But my husband," she points to the parking lot with her thumb, "he grew up in the Midwest. This will be the first time he or the kids have seen the ocean, except for in books and magazines—things like that. He's always telling me that he'd like to live the rest of his life on a boat—catching sharks and stuff." She ducks her head and leans a little closer to Ajay, like she is about to tell him something in confidence. "But I think he reads too many National Geographics."

The woman straightens and screws her mouth to one side. "The East Coast is okay, I guess. But I'd like to see California."

Even though there are no spills, Ajay wipes the counter with a damp cloth out of habit. He smiles at the woman, a mass of white teeth against dark, clear skin.

"My brother lives in Norman, Oklahoma," he says.

I remember that Ajay has eleven brothers and sisters.

***

The hamburgers arrive through a small access way that connects the restaurant's kitchen to the counter in the dining room. Ajay stacks them carefully in a brown paper bag. Grease stains appear almost instantly on the bottom and sides of the sack. The woman beckons the boys to the counter to help her.

"Take this bag and the lemonades to the car," she says, and they skip on ahead, ready to eat. The little girl takes her mother's hand and they too head for the door. The woman turns and looks at Ajay mopping the counter. "Maybe I will see you again, someday."

Her phrase lingers in my ears. This was the first thought that came to my mind the day after, when I found it too much effort to lift my head from the pillow.

Toola replaces my drink as I glance at my watch.

By now you would be finishing up the back nine and meeting me at The Anchors-Inn for a drink; then we would bring brownies or a piece of pie they keep under a glass dome on the counter to share on the boat. Apple if it were your turn to choose, cherry if it were mine.

Why don't I tell Toola? Toola, who has been so kind to us over the years, Toola who would frown and give me a big hug and pat my hand with tears in her eyes. Maybe I will invite her home with me someday. I can serve her iced tea swimming with lemon and hibiscus leaves and give her a tour of our house. We can sit on the sofas I have re-upholstered with white slipcovers that I have wanted for years.

Too impractical, you argued. The only time you ever put your foot down.

But it is the explanation that I am avoiding, leaving me with two choices: come clean with the truth or never come here again because word will eventually get out. Right now, I think it would be easier to leave and never return.

***

Outside, the kids crawl into the back seat of the station wagon. The woman shields her eyes from the sun and looks for her husband in the parking lot. He has been absorbed by the activity in the marina but turns as if by telepathy and strides toward the car. I can see the husband and wife speaking to each other and then the man heads for the restaurant.

A bell over the door rings when he enters. It rings for every customer although it is the first time I have noticed it today. The man goes straight for the bar and speaks to Ajay in a low voice.

Ajay sets a shot down on the counter, and the man does not waste any time tipping his head back, drinking the amber liquid. He speaks again to Ajay and then he also heads for the washroom. I watch as Ajay pours another shot and sets it beside the man's first glass. I wonder if the woman knows that her husband is drinking.

Didn't I get mad when you would come here from the course, and I could smell the whiskey on your breath? I would warn you: 'Only one more.' And you would grin and say, 'Don't worry, Marta, I will be careful,' using your Finnish mother's pet name for me.

My fingers need a manicure. I gave them color just this morning, a sparkly bronze shade I chose from the Rite Aid back home. But I have been chipping the polish off little by little as I take in my surroundings at the bar. I sweep the flakes of polish discreetly on the floor with the back of my hand when I think no one is looking. They glitter like fool's gold and blend in with the sand from the flip flops of the tourists and the fishermen's rubber boots. There is always sand on the floor here—gray, coarse, and dry—and no matter how many times it is swept away, it creeps back inside like a midnight intruder.

After you died, and before your mother boarded the plane back to Savonlinna, she put one hand on both sides of my head. "Marta, you must go forward," she reminded me in halting English. "Only memories live in the past."

I boldly skirt the truth twice this week. Katie, my neighbor next door, caught me on the front lawn yesterday looking for the morning paper only for me to realize that I had neglected to renew our summer subscription.

"It's so good to see you guys back. Summer must be truly here!" she gushes, waving her hands wildly over her head. "Can you believe this weather?"

I nod in agreement but don't correct her by informing that 'we' are not back for the summer, that now I am here alone. I pacify myself by claiming guilt only by omission.

At the Village Grocer, I bump into Mrs. Long who mentions that she didn't see you drive in with me on Saturday afternoon. I tell her that you will be arriving later in the month, and I mention something about you having to work another week or two in the city. The words quickly slip off my tongue before I have the chance to swallow them, as if my lying mouth has a life of its own.

***

Toola nods and winks at me. I think she is pointing to my glass, and I hold up a finger for one more. She shakes her head slightly and points discreetly outside, indicating something going on behind me. I turn to see the station wagon with the Oklahoma tags peeling out of the parking lot; the wheels scuffing up their own version of a Mid-Western dust bowl.

The man does not seem to realize that he has been deserted when he returns from the restroom. He strides to the bar and swallows his second shot quickly but takes his time fiddling for a billfold in the back pocket of his khakis as if he is in no hurry to resume his journey. He hands Ajay some money for the shots of liquor and lays a bill on the counter for a tip.

A BOSTONIAN

Lorri Ventura

His home is a rag-filled refrigerator box
Propped crookedly on broken sidewalk
Alongside the Boston Common

When I ask his name
He says, "Just call me
'Least of Your Brothers,'"
Then winks conspiratorially

He tugs off mismatched gloves
To jab his raw fingers
Into his tepid cup of Dunkin'
Before gulping its dregs
Coffee trickles through his beard
As he offers a sip to a passerby
Who squawks in protest
Before bolting to the other side of Tremont Street

The gold-gilded State House dome
Shines down on him
As his gnarled fingers weave gently
Through the yarn hair
Of the grimy, one-eyed Raggedy Ann

Propped in his lap

Every so often

He leans forward and kisses the top of the doll's

Head with a sweetness that brings tears to my eyes

Seeing people turn their faces away

As they rush past him

Pretending they don't see them

He waves and grins lopsidedly

Pushing his tongue through three wobbly teeth and chortling,

"Smile! I won't hurt you! Have a good day!"

I squint through the sunlight

As I watch him from the nearest corner

And I think I see

A halo encircling his head

THE PATH NOT WANTED

Kathleen A Rogers

I hear Kate's soft voice in the next room as she plays with our grandson. Here, within my curtained room, I pretend to watch them. Imagining is a way to share life beyond this makeshift room. Kate had insisted that I not spend my last days alone in a hospital or hidden away in our bedroom. She and my daughter converted the dining room into a bedroom of sorts, a place where I could be surrounded with family and my books which line the walls. The windows are covered with pictures and stories the grandkids have made for me. Some say "Get Well." They do not yet understand.

Here, I now lie dying. Once in my youth, I sought a path to learn what motivated the soul of man. My quest to understand, to make a difference is now nearly over. What difference have I really made? Was I wrong to have searched for paths which led me beyond my reach, or should I have been content after college with my 9 to 5 job and a house in pleasant suburbia? How egotistical to have thought one could grasp what men far greater than me had not! But, there always has been—there still is this madness in me: the need to seek, to know, to understand. The dreams of the stretching continents still gnaw inside me. Always, there was this unrelenting desire to get close to the Earth—to know its people and share that knowledge through my writing.

Always, there was more to see, more to know, more to share. What I learned was never enough! I wrote for the Associated Press about my walks through the streets of Newark after the riots and of my talks with men darker than me. I listened to their shattered dreams, and wrote of the chains which still held them. But what did it change?

Oh, once I almost did find the answer to my yearning, find my path to make a difference. I went to Vietnam as a civilian, not a soldier. I was not willing to fight in a war I thought wrong, but I needed to understand, to be a witness. I needed to comprehend what led men to risk their lives for those they did not know. I never did. But I absorbed their fear through the sound of bombs rumbling through the night and got to know the wounded land of war. I witnessed the depth of humanity through both small and large gestures, through words to loved ones back home—words traveling through the phone lines I'd helped install. For a few, I'd made a difference, but the war still went on, men still died, and children still huddled in fear. So little changed! Where was God?

I sought the meaning of God on the beaches of Borneo as I watched the changing spectrum of color in the sunsets—a song of hues in the silence, a hymn to God. I sought His message in the tranquility of a Buddhist temple in Taiwan, in the vast silence of the desert, and in the lingering chants of monks of yore. The echo of their voices still rise in the mist to the chapel on the hill.

I abandoned my search—no, "just a slight detour," was my thought. I had confidence in time and life back then. I was sure that I could accomplish my dreams—all of them and more. But I needed first to return to Kate. Marriage had never been part of my plan. Settling down was not part of my vision. I'd fought against it for more than a year. Then, at some inexplicable moment, *like* became *love*. I needed her beside me, her sense of humor, her intellectual curiosity, her love of books and ideas. I needed her grounding—which was the very thing I also feared the most. I knew instinctively that only she could make me whole. That wholeness would sustain me for the rest of my life, especially when our bodies folded into each other at night—heartbeats becoming one.

Even after we married, I could not stop looking, propelled always by my inner need to know. Kate remained true to her promise and allowed me to continue my search beyond well-worn paths, adjusting her career as I did so. She went with me to live in Europe. We explored the cathedrals together, and marveled at the endurance of human will that had constructed them brick by brick so many years ago. Was it man's need to create, or his love of God that made him build such structures? Perhaps, the two could not be separated.

Back home in the States, Kate stayed behind as I pursued my quest one summer with the Inuits. I wrote, "I went to find, if I could, what thing it could be that holds men there in a place where desolation is the neighborhood." Watching them weave together their old culture with the new, I understood better man's ability to adapt. I wrote how one became part of the flat open spaces, a part of the landscape. Returning home, at first, the noise and crowds overwhelmed me, left me yearning for that place of desolation.

Only once did Kate say a definitive "no" to my searches. I had been offered a grant to take my family to follow a Bedouin group for a year through the desert. (We had three children by then.) "You may go alone," she'd said. "It's too dangerous for the children." Of course, she was right. I stayed. Several years later, I met the man who took my place. He'd been lost, separated from civilization for two years. He did not share what he had learned.

Ironically, the past thirty plus years have been spent in that suburbia I ran from so long ago. Family responsibilities gradually limited my seeking and learning to the books which line my walls. Old quests and dreams were left unanswered, tucked away. I have left but brief impressions on this earth.

Kate is near now. I feel her presence just behind the make-shift curtain door. She pulls the curtain open. "You are awake. You must be thirsty." I'm not, but I sip the juice she gives me. Her voice is a signal, and they troop in—in small groups, or one by one, laughing, telling stories, playing music for me. I listen to them, my two daughters and two sons—strong, successful, compassionate adults. I hear the grandchildren giggling as they are herded downstairs. There are the others, too, who come and go—brother, sisters, friends—the parade of my life before me.

"Does my search for the meaning of life end now?" I wonder. "Or, at last, will I find my answers as my body dissolves into the Earth—mingling with the bones of other souls who have gone before?" Then, I realize that perhaps the path not wanted is the very one that holds all the answers. They're found in the laughter of friends, the beauty of my children's souls, and the steady hand of the woman who made me whole.

WOMAN IN A NURSING HOME

Lorri Ventura

The skin on the backs of her hands

Looks like lady slipper petals

Translucent

Tiny-veined

So delicate

She scratches it incessantly

Buckled into a wheelchair

By the elevator door

In front of the nurses' station

Which is where the staff

Park the patients who don't get visitors

Threadbare pate pitched forward

Stained hospital gown

Doing its job half-heartedly

Covering body parts

That are faded memories

Of what they once were

Seemingly asleep

Until the elevator doors

Whisper their announcement

Of someone's arrival

Then, only then

Does she become animated

Her head lifts

Her smile is almost rictal

"Hi hi hi hi hi!"

She sing-songs

"See me!"

Her unspoken plea

I bend down

And carefully embrace her

Telling her she looks pretty today

Her fingers catch in my hair

Her skin smells like

Chicken grease

Rheumy eyes lock on mine

"Bless you bless you bless you!"

She warbles

It feels like a long time passes

Before we release each other

I think she just might be

The most perfect human being

I've ever met

DORIS
Excerpt from *Just Everyday People*

Les Clark

I met Doris, a truly gentle, wonderful woman, with an angelic visage. When her hair was backlit, it created a halo. She came into my life when she rounded the bases for the 99th time and was still able to get around with a walker. She was on my route when I worked for a social service agency, daily delivering hot meals to her apartment in a modern retirement facility.

As aging took its toll—mobility, meal prep, personal needs—the family moved her to an assisted-living community where she received supportive, attentive care. Her social worker, initial J, is appropriately, a joy.

I visited Doris on an early September day. She was now 101, chair bound, suffering the lost mobility of her right leg. As I sat with her at noon, Doris was lucid, smiling—her ever present, large-print book angled for her daily reading pleasure. I always got a happy greeting. "Well, hello," she said enthusiastically. "Have you learned how to play backgammon?" She politely left off "yet." She had been challenging me for months.

After some mutual chitchat, catching up on what I was doing and how each of us was feeling, she related an upcoming cortisone shot in her hip to alleviate nagging pain. "They have to take me by ambulance. I can't get into a car anymore."

I love sitting with my friend, but I was unprepared for the following soliloquy.

I dreamt about dying two nights in a row last week. I was okay with it.

I remember when my son Jim was dying, not in the dream, but in real life. If you remember, I told you Jim was a paraplegic all his life. We were all around his bed, all his brothers and sisters. I was 100 and he was 75. I told him we were all happy, we could be there with him. I held his hand as he took his last breath.

In my dream, everyone was with me as I was dying. And I was okay with it.

Doris finished with, "I'm ready to go."

I was speechless.

Her story ending, Doris gave me a crooked smile. "Can you push my lunch table over? They give me so much food. Breakfast was just at nine. Coffee and orange juice and oatmeal and eggs and toast and water. Now this." Not unlike James Bond in License to Kill, she had a license to complain.

Doris beckoned me close. As I bent near, she held my face and gave me an air kiss.

THE ROAD NOT TAKEN

James Thibeault

As Harmony was pulled by her two dogs down a small path in the woods, she couldn't get the stupid poem by Robert Frost out of her head.

After some effect, she managed to yank on her dogs' leashes hard enough to get them to finally stop dragging her through the muddy trail. The cold, wet February was the worst time of the year to take out Molly and Maggy through the woods behind her house. However, it was a thousand times better than taking the pitbulls down Main Street that not only had no sidewalks, but also a never ending parade of tractor trailers that scared the shit out of them. Instead, her excited pups would divulge themselves in dirt while her new Puma's would have to be wiped down again. Finally, she had enough of their delight when the trail broke off into two. She stared at two paths: her typical route with the dogs, and the less-traveled, unkempt, tick-infested shithole that had the pitbulls wagging their tails.

"Fuck Robert Frost …" thought Harmony—remembering the line: *Two roads diverged in a yellow wood.*

"Girls, I don't want to go down there," Harmony said. Their leashes remained taut, their snouts pointing in one direction. Harmony knew the dogs could easily overpower her at any second. "I'm not playing around. Either we go down the regular path, or we take our chances with the 18-wheelers—do you want that?" Molly sneezed in response, which was difficult to discern as a *yes* or *no*. Maggy sniffed Molly's butt—which seemed like a more fitting answer.

In college, she used to have Frost's poem taped to her wall. No frame, just a printed single sheet paper with the poem in size 30 font. She kept it beside her bed, so when she woke up, Harmony would subconsciously "take the road less traveled." For her, this meant "roads" less traveled for herself. For example, instead of her daily boring cereal for breakfast in the dining hall, she'd try a spinach and feta omelet. Or, instead of spending Saturday night finishing her essay on Maya Angelou, she accepted a friend's invite to a frat party. Instead of finally finishing the last book of The Mists of Avalon series, she slept with Owen.

Her choices certainly "made all the difference". She gained weight because feta apparently equals fat, she never even came close to magna cum laude, and Owen and Harmony were married after college—adopting two fur babies soon afterwards. Happy home, happy life—except Owen couldn't find time to take the dogs out. He fucking works at home, but the first thing that Harmony has to do when she gets home is change to her Pumas and walk the pitbulls. "I got conferences. I don't know what to tell you" was the constant response from her husband. The poor dogs immediately went on the front yard because they were holding it so long. This was a huge pain because that involved using the poo bags since nothing could happen to Owen's precious lawn. If the girls went into the woods, Harmony could easily just flick the remains off the trail with a stick.

Molly and Maggy looked back at Harmony with their stupidly adorable faces. "Stop being so goddamn cute," Harmony said, "It's the only thing stopping me from hating both of you right now." They kept looking at the trail and back to her. Deep down, Harmony wanted to venture down that less-traveled road again. She wanted to change up her diet, study hard to get a new job, and divorce Owen. But changes have consequences, and many of her decisions had unknown effects— some lasting many long years. Sure, this path that the dogs wanted to go on might be fun and exciting, but then there would be ticks. Then, Owen would stand by watching, orating stupid advice, while she somehow tried to remove pests from squirming muscular dogs with tiny tweezers.

"You're a dead white man who doesn't know shit," said Harmony surprisingly loudly. It startled the pups to the point where they stopped fidgeting. Instead, they bowed their heads and ceased wagging their tails. Harmony bent down and took turns rubbing both of the girls—trying to hold back her tears. The dogs licked her face and pointed their snouts in the other direction. Together, they took the road most traveled.

GO GO DANCER

Aidan Needle

Plastic heels on linoleum, up

on heaven's disco floor. Scuffed by the passing blue

man who understands how priceless your boots are, but offers a cup

of lemonade tea for repair, and you don't want to, but you can't argue

with a customer. He sits and reads you Ginsberg—says he's a beatnik,

which should be a warning to get the fuck out of there.

So you stumble those broken boots across the cover band's loose picks

to the backroom. You need a new outfit to wear.

'Cause the men in the crowd will scream

if you don't open that velveteen curtain in calf-length

zip-ups. Stomping out like a Fleetwood Mac coke dream--

dancing on the radio wavelengths.

I'm in the crowd,

watching those orange boots kick to some vintage song

all the boys know, it makes you proud.

Wishing I wasn't some poet because I never belonged.

Not like you do here.

I want to be a gogo dancer after a night. Early morning on the pier

The way I'd love to sparkle as the waves crash in on high tide.

OFF THE BEATEN PATH

Sharon Ann Harmon

the covid world
feels off kilter
like one hand clapping

we watch the news
inundated with sorrow
or we don't watch and feel
alienated from others

our arms ache
for a hug from a child
parent or friend

we miss people and places
that were never on our radar
our dreams hang heavy
in the air

the taste of anxiety always

on our lips

the bitterness of fear

in the back of our throats

the lonesomeness of one flower

in the desert

Previously published online at The Straw Dog Writers' Guild.

SPLASH FROM THE PAST

Phyllis Cochran

Why do children love to stomp, splash in, and slog through puddles? You turn your head for a second, and they race for the nearest one. No matter how many times Mom yells, "You're getting wet. Stay out of the water," it's hard to convince a little one to walk away.

While growing up in the country, I recall hot summer days. At the first sign of a sprinkle, we slipped into bathing suits and darted outside to await the downpour. Then we'd dance around in roadside puddles and squeeze our feet in the soggy grass. What fun! Our visiting city cousins joined us one particular afternoon and squealed when a lizard slithered across our path.

It isn't just puddles that entice children. The river too often beckoned us when we were young. My younger sister, Carol, and cousin Harriet spent days gathering planks, tying ropes, pounding nails in an effort to build a raft, with plans to ride down the shallow river flowing past our home. When invited to view their craft and watch this grand journey, I stood on the shore wondering how far they would float. Their dream of riding the current died when they hopped aboard. The raft immediately sank. Standing knee-deep in the murky water, I saw their discouragement.

Although, as adults, we act a bit more reserved and do our best to sidestep puddles, I've noticed several people deliberately tiptoe through them. My friend, Kathy, recently admitted that when she and her husband, John, find a puddle, they still love splashing each other.

Maybe some of us outgrow the puddle syndrome, but we gravitate toward water in other settings. In awe, we gaze at the ocean surf. Closing our eyes, we sniff the salty air, listening to the breaking of waves against the rocky coast of Maine. Even calmer bodies of water draw us close by teasing us with their rippling sounds.

Niagara Falls is another amazing sight. While driving across the country years ago, I wondered why water has the tendency to captivate us. While touring Pennsylvania, a billboard loomed up along the highway. In bold lettering, we read, "Ruby Falls—Pennsylvania's answer to Niagara Falls."

Not able to resist, my husband Phil and I drove to the tourist attraction, departing a bit disappointed. We had anticipated a more powerful display. But the experience did not dampen our attraction to water. During another road trip, I marveled at the magnitude of rivers that we viewed from the car. In the New Mexico Visitors' Guidebook, we noted a suggested scenic tour. Of course, I was hooked by Nambe Pueblo Falls along the route.

The following day, we rode over paved and bumpy dirt roads on an Indian reservation, eventually hiking upward through the woods to view the sight. Huffing and puffing due to the elevation level (not because we were out of shape), we rested. Nearing the overlook, I listened for the familiar rush. Due to lack of rain, Nambe Pueblo Falls merely trickled over the rocky bed below. If this trek seemed futile, the small stream below grabbed my attention. Stooping over, I swished my hands around, tossed a stone into the stream and waited for the plop before heading for the car.

When was the last time you lingered near or rode by a stream, brook, pond, or lake? Did you feel the urge to test the temperature of the water with your hands or toes? If you did, was it refreshing? Maybe not if you attempted this as I did in mid-September in the icy Atlantic Ocean of Hampton Beach.

Do you wonder if you're the only one who experiences water in a particular way? When you look around, observe or hear other people's comments, you realize that you're not so different after all.

My sister-in-law, Joyce, insisted we see Anna Ruby Falls in the Georgia Mountains. Immediately she glanced at the riverbed along the pathway and announced, "I'd like to put my feet in the water."

She spoke aloud the words that I was thinking. This time the falls were satisfying. Dynamically, the thunderous torrent rushed forcefully down over the rugged cliffs. What a sight!

One year, our niece, Nancy, came from Arizona. She visited us during a summer break from college. Rain poured down in torrents one afternoon. Hardly able to wait for the rain to stop, Nancy slipped off her shoes, ran to the back lawn, and danced in bare feet—squeezing the wet grass between her toes.

Standing and watching from the window, I couldn't help thinking about nature's beauty and its effect. For those brief minutes, the cares of the world fade. Faith soars. To remain in this atmosphere, contemplating our surroundings, would be ecstasy.

The puddles of our childhood, the sensation of a summer's rain on our faces, the coldness of the ocean around our ankles, our hands swishing, or toes wiggling in a lake seem to free us to enjoy these everyday treasures that otherwise escape us. In those fleeting moments, we are uninhibited, allowed to let go. In this peaceful state, we gain a greater perspective of God's gifts created for our pleasure.

Now I understand why children love puddles.

Previously published in Country Essence Magazine in August, 2004

SHADOW PEOPLE

Michael Young

A dismal drizzle

slickened the country road

as I drove past

one of the shadow people,

vague of age,

indiscriminate gender.

Stringy hair streamed out

beneath hat brim,

down soaked duster.

His beard visible

just in passing.

I saw him

headed for a fire

beneath a railroad bridge,

a tent with a tarp

in a hobo camp.

Some place warm and dry.

In other times,

Grandpa would have

picked him up,

taken him back to the farm,

given him a good meal and

let him earn his keep

doing the chores –

until time to move on.

But romance has gone out of

riding the rails,

jumping off as the train

slows at the RR crossing,

tramping across the tracks

where the Union Pacific and

Northern Pacific lie side by side

along small town Front Street.

Praising Jesus in the

Front Street Mission

seems too much to pay for a

shower, a hot, and a cot.

Unless you already

love Jesus!

Now, even CEOs bunk in

the back of a Buick or

seek shelter beneath

the umbrella of Chapter 11.

The best you can hope for

in bad times are

some really good folk songs.

Where are our

Pastures of Plenty,

Rolling Mills of New Jersey,

Fertile Fields of California?

Where have all the songsters gone?

Utah Phillips,

Pete Seeger,

Woody Guthrie -

where are you?

We need you

now!

AIN'T NO MOUNTAIN HIGH ENOUGH

Allan Fournier

She looked 'cross the mountain
and what did she see?
Mike trudging along
with his family:

There's Ben on one side,
and Zach on the other,
Danielle was right there,
along with their mother.

Mike was waging two battles:
Parkinson's, oh brother;
the other was taking
one step ... then another.

Those steps would take him
all the way to the top
of Mount Washington! Yes!
In this quest, he did ... not ... stop.

"Inspire." A word
that gets bandied about,

but it happened that day;
of that—have no doubt.

It planted a seed
in the heart of my sister;
and hey, when that happens,
there's no stoppin' her, mister!

She became a "peak bagger",
a real hiker, mate.
In New Hampshire the count
is yikes—forty eight!

And oh, did I mention,
before you go try—
they must be at least
four thousand feet high!

She hiked and she hiked.
She bagged one by one.
Out with Mother Nature,
she had lots of fun.

But also she battled
against Parkinson's.
One step ... then another,
for awareness and funds.

45, 46,

47, and then,

the last "where" was known,

but the weather (#?/!)—oh when?

Sunday, August 20,

her birthday, ya' know,

and the "where" was the mountain ...

her last name, Monroe.

She called upon family

and friends young and old.

Here's the list of those hikers,

if I may be so bold:

Her son, Bradley T,

and his girl, known as Jade;

there's Rick and there's Karen,

good friends she has made.

Allan and Mickey

and daughter Marie,

and then Brian D

and his girl, Allie.

Brian's dad, Jim

our cheerleader—yay!

and last but not least,

there comes Brian J.

Tara wanted to come,

would've been, with a smile;

but priority one

was to walk … down the aisle.

They made it to Bretton,

in spirit on trail,

our P. D. team captains,

that's them, Mike and Gail!

We counted twelve hikers,

and then off we went.

At the end we must have

at least 90 percent!

To show up their elders,

they'll do what they must.

The youngin's they left

us old farts in the dust!

But every so often

we'd all group together.

You know what they say

about "birds of a feather".

The water refreshing,
the views straight from heaven.
I hope that our count
isn't down to eleven!

Back on the trail,
our cheer we would croon.
More on that later,
more on that soon.

Then before ya' know it:
Here's the hut! Here's the top!
Let's celebrate and …
take pictures non-stop!

As this poem winds down …
it is time for a cheer.
So all gather 'round—
come, come, here! here!

Now fill up your lungs,
and with no hesitation,
just belt it on out:
Go Team … Domin … Achin!

WAITING

Phyllis Cochran

Hours creep by slowly
Darkness sweeps the air
Those in white keep passing
We just wait and stare.

Oh why must time enslave us,
Bind us to this day?
We yearn within to take our flight
Instead we wait and pray.

Were we chosen to sit alone
From morn to eventide,
To ask ourselves the question
Why do we wait here inside?

Only God who spoke the word
Can change our destiny
Ease our aching hearts
Come and set us free.

PILGRIM ON THE PATH

as told by Pir Vilayat Inayat Khan
retold by Michael Young

There once was a pilgrim on the path searching for a teacher. He heard of a special master who lived in a far-a-way valley in the shadow of a majestic mountain. One day, with little in his possession other than his thirst for spiritual knowledge, he trudged to the home of the Master.

Upon his arrival, he spied the master with his flowing robes and his long, white beard. Prostrating himself at his feet, the pilgrim implored, "Oh most noble Master, please take me as your disciple! I would do anything to sit at your feet and learn from you."

"Very well, Pilgrim" replied the Master, "tend my roses."

It was then that the Pilgrim realized he was in the most elegant of rose gardens, with bushes of many varieties of the most fragrant blossoms he had ever seen. Under the direction of the Master, he learned to cultivate and prune the roses. The Pilgrim was given special prayers and spiritual practices to recite while caring for the magnificent flowers. He even learned to call them by their names, some quite exotic and foreign. There was the dark Damascus Rose, the Venetian Rose that came via the Silk Road, and the Royal Rose of the Indian sheik, Nur Jehan.

In the cool of the evening, the Pilgrim would sit at the seat of the Master and listen to his teaching, often in the company of other devoted disciples who lived nearby or in the small monastery on the property. This went on for quite some time. But the Pilgrim was never invited into the temple that sat just up from the rose garden. Only in the temple could the Pilgrim be initiated into the inner circle. Then, he would be able to sit with the senior monks and receive advanced lessons.

One day, the Pilgrim got up the courage to address his Master.

"Oh Master, for these many days have I tended your rose garden with prayers and spiritual practices, and yet I have never been invited into the temple with your other disciples. What must I do to gain entrance into the temple?"

With that, the Master handed him a sack and a spade, and pointed to the neighboring mountain.

"My son, if you would enter the temple, you must first take this sack to the mountain. There is a large cave in which you will find something that my roses love and need to flourish."

The Pilgrim took the large sack and a small spade, along with a meager loaf of bread and flask of water, and scaled the mountain path. Before him loomed the mouth of a vast cave. As he was about to enter, there issued forth from the cave's mouth a dark cloud of bats! Though startled, the Pilgrim was still determined to enter the cave for the sake of his Master and the beloved roses. It was then that he was overcome by the putrid stench of what lay inside on the cave floor.

There must be some mistake!

Abruptly, the Pilgrim whirled around and hurried back down the mountain. Panting for breath, he returned to the garden, where he dropped the sack and slumped dejectedly to the ground before his Master.

"Oh Master, please forgive me! I have done as you asked but could not take anything from the cave. Do you know what those bats are depositing on its floor? It's disgusting!"

"Yes, my son. I know, but you have not done as I instructed. It is what my roses love, what feeds them." With that, the Master picked up the empty sack and handed it back to the Pilgrim. "If you would enter the temple, you must first learn to deal with bats and the fertile excrement on the floor of the cave."

DARK WOODS

Jon Bishop

There are whispers in the trees—

or are they voices?

It's hard to tell in these woods,

with pitch-darkness all around.

Sounds lose all grounding.

The cracks of branches underfoot

could be people, at a distance,

coming toward you,

ready to join you on your midnight hike

or to do you harm.

All life, here and now, is through a glass,

darkly, Saint Paul says.

But despite this, you push forward.

We all do. And soon, you're climbing

the tower you were here to climb,

the one just beyond the woods,

the one built by the billionaire

who used to live in this town,

who collected bricks and stacked them,

one by one, until he, finished, looked up

and saw that he had pierced time

and nature and the sky,

and now you, at the top,

can see the entire city laid bare,

can smash the present moment,

can stare at life itself made visible.

THE LIDO DECK
Excerpt from
JUST EVERYDAY PEOPLE :

Les Clark

That's what we call it, but it was really my neighbor's weathered grey back porch, soon facing conversion into a three-season escape for two friends. Well, he had talked of screening it in—we had also been talking about it for years, and we'd been having weekend drinks together.

We think it is the closest we will *ever* get to the aft of some luxury liner, waitstaff attending to our every idiotic whim, frothy concoctions on shining silver trays, white linens over bent arms.

"I'll have another, if you please, and may I have two umbrellas this time?"

My friend's back deck, once a vibrant forest green, had transitioned in New England weather to a sad, streaked grey, like a bad combover. We knew better than to walk barefoot. These battered planks were dotted with deck chairs—those cheap white resin jobs we pretended were cushy chaises with colorful cushions. We sometimes sat there in the rain, often forgetting if we'd gotten wet. Mixed drinks had that effect.

Beyond the deck, his two red maples provided cooling shade during steamy summer days. On the other side of our mutual fence was *my* tree. Like *Prince,* it is of unknown breed. My friend keeps threatening, under the cover of night, to cut it down because it served as a ladder for the squirrel families scampering up the bark highway, leaping onto his garage roof. Squirrels aren't bachelors. We suspect there may be generations living in the rafters. I argue their cuteness—he argues the demise of my shrub-cum-tree.

We usually end the arguments with a toast.

At the far end of the deck is a flowering Rose of Sharon. The flowers are a stunning deep blue and violet. It has been moved all over his yard and mine. It took two summers to decide on the first move, long before arthritis turned us into the Tin Woodmen.

The Lido Deck is a respite, an oasis at week's end regardless of the season. As our friendship matured, we found a mutual fondness for Manhattans, or anything brewed with hops and barley. We had no brand loyalty. The only requirements were cheap, cold, and straight from the can. I occasionally supplied a local microbrew whose label displayed a railroad logo, honoring my friend's model railroading hobby—or if it said "beer."

His other skills were cooking and baking. On those nights, I supplied my appetite. We got surprisingly good preparing steamers with an attendant mirepoix broth. Butter, whether store brand or Irish, helped round out his porch table straining under the load. The rules of the Lido Deck mandated sharing, however our shrewd timing somehow did not sync with other foodies.

Most of the time though, it was a chance for a couple of guys to talk about the day's events, local and world, or how (when) we were going to get projects done. That screening thing—one of these days.

MINE FOR THE AFTERNOON

Phyllis Cochran

The door hardly closes behind me when Paxton, my childrens' Puggle, bounds down the stairs and leaps up to greet me. His tan ears tilt backwards. Large brown eyes brighten as he stares adoringly up into my face. Pax is graying around his nose and behind his ears now. We are aging together. Pax and I have a special rapport. We savor our time each afternoon while family members work.

"You're coming with Granny for our walk," I say. Pax wags his tail, races to the living room, and rolls over on his back for me to rub his tummy. This is important. He is testing me to see if I really care. I bend over, satisfy him with a couple of scratches, and we're off.

"Today is beautiful. We'll drive to the track." Pax's ears perk up. Obediently, he sits upright in the passenger side of the car, staring straight ahead. I reach over and pat him.

Arriving at the bike track, he whimpers his happy whimper, letting me know he can't wait to spring free from the car and begin sniffing. Of course, it's all about sniffing, and I'm prepared to walk at a leisurely pace while he finds the right spot to empty himself. I yank on his leash from time to time. He is more engrossed in scents than moving forward.

We're in full view of a pond where Canada geese are swimming. "No, Pax, not with Granny. No swimming with me," I say sternly. He's eager to race down the embankment and leap into the water to paddle around. Choosing my footing downward over rough terrain will never happen. Once I missed a step on a stony beach incline. I found myself sprinting downward and dived headlong, nose-first onto a bed of stones. Never again, I tell myself.

I clench Paxton's leash when he picks up the pace. Thankfully, benches along the course invite me to sit and catch my breath, as do other walkers with their dogs. Pax can't wait to meet new friends and gives me the opportunity to strike up conversations with strangers.

Bikes fly by. Mothers wheeling babies catch up to us on this leisurely stroll. Pax needs coaxing to turn around. "Who's hungry? Who needs a snack?" My luring doesn't always work. Pax has a strong will. I pull him across the track to reverse directions. Soon, Pax leads the way toward the parking lot. I pick up speed to keep up with his pace.

After our lunchtime nibbles, we rest for a while back in my home. Paxton hops into his favorite chair by the window overlooking the street. Here, he barks at anyone passing by with their dogs.

Busy with household chores, I lose track of time. But my buddy begins telling me it's dinner time. He knows when it's five o'clock. He follows me around, staring until he has my complete attention. "Okay! Okay! Give me a minute." I tell him. He eyes his food in my hand and prances about.

In one gulp, the food is gone, and the plate licked clean. Racing to his toy basket, Pax returns with a long squeaky toy animal nearly torn to shreds. He always wins this tug of war game. I decide to toss a ball, and we play chase the ball for a while until I am weary. Pax resorts to the army crawl as if to say, *look how cute I am.* How can I not be taken in by my companion? I lean over to pat him. He rolls over for another tummy rub.

After playtime, Pax takes his position sitting upright in his chair. He turns his head and focuses on the outside door listening and waiting for footsteps or the sound of a familiar car. He seems to know when his special someone arrives long before I hear a car door close.

On evenings if family members are late picking him up, he lays down and glares at the door. When the phone rings for a report to explain why no one has retrieved Paxton, his ears perk up. He looks quizzically toward me and listens to my conversation. I hang up, and he continues waiting with his ears forward and eyes directed to me for information. The only way to keep him calm and let him know what is happening is to say, "One minute." I must not say the words Mark or Momma, or Pax will race to the door expecting they are here for him. I speak to my pal and say, "They said, 'One minute.'" These two words have multiple meanings. It can mean he needs to stay longer and cannot readily leave. Minutes or hours might pass before we see the door open. He must wait longer. Paxton understands the message. He settles down.

Mark eventually shows up. He is Pax's favorite. He hardly sits before Pax is in his lap, licking his face and snuggling with him.

"He's smiling," Mark says. If dogs smile, I agree. This is the closest to a smile.

My time is finished until tomorrow when Paxton again is mine for the afternoon.

SUGAR HIGH

Cecilia Januszewski

furry insects, my teeth,

clicking and buzzing, shine

like wet hair

sweet insects, mind you,

sweetness and noise,

licking my lips and slithering down my tongue sucking my molars

and rubbing against my gums

my jaw (how it aches), my jaw,

from beating wings.

Wings

and the sweet noise of legs,

twitching and spinning,

that sings

PATHWAYS OF ADVENTURE

Travel, Local, and Nature Writing

WALKING ON QUABBIN

William Doreski

Deerflies snarling in my hair,

I wander down to the reservoir,

the largest in New England,

and kneel on the pebble shore

and drink a great baptismal draught

and pretend I'm whole again,

as Robert Frost promised I'd be.

The huge sprawl of water conceals

entire drowned villages: church,

houses, post office, general store.

I'd like to walk the muddy roads

and peer into windows and watch

drowned citizens eating lunch,

listening to the radio, shopping

for milk and flour in cotton sacks.

Maybe I'd hear them sing a hymn

or catch them making babies

the way people always do.

But no one drowned, no one walks

under or on the water unless

I do. The shine looks gelatinous.

Maybe I can persuade myself,
so I try one step and feel
the entire reservoir toughen
like half-cured concrete. Another
step, gingerly, and another,
and soon I'm twenty feet from shore
and walking on water the way

my ancestors did while evolving
in a mist of DNA. Below
I see the wreck of a village
the houses, church steeple swaying
like a lily stem. People swagger
among the schools of minnows,
their overalls and cotton dresses

crisp as if freshly dry-cleaned.
They look up at me, point and laugh,
and I realize how foolish
I look, walking on their atmosphere
with my rubber soles, so I turn
back to shore and stop pretending
silly old miracles can save.

UNDER SURVEILLANCE

Dee Matthews

Three crows on a limb

scold me as I stroll

beneath them, then beyond

their cathedral of the pines.

Preach, preach, preach at me;

proclaim their territory.

Vigilant black eyes

never blink on their watch

as I trespass on up the hill,

over the stonewall, then

disappear from their decree.

WARE RIVER

William Doreski

Below Quabbin, the Ware River
pours through a rain-swept wilderness.
The brown current scallops and quivers.
Chunks of good earth tumble downstream.
With a few other tourists
I hike the official trails
in search of epiphany.

A park ranger suggests the path
to the right, up a ledge of granite and beyond.
We trace this path to a fieldstone
slate-roofed house
with a tall view of the river.
Inside, a brass bed, fresh linen,
and a wall furnace breathing heat
so dry our rain-soak instantly dissipates.

Someone famous died here,
a desperate artist rumpled with age,
withdrawn in river-meditation,
his favorite lover dead,
his canvases turned to the wall.

We feel his ghost pass through us
as we gaze at the river.
Below the house, it seems to broaden
like the sea, an illusion
of mist and cloud and tumbled light.

The others sigh and begin the hike
to the road, but I linger to read
the titles of books beside the bed.
Abruptly I'm in the bed, wrestling
with a silken muscular woman
whose mouth pouts like a starfish,
her gin-breath overpowering,
her portraits stored in the basements
of museums in Paris, Brussels, Milan.

The little house darkens.
The river crashes through the windows
and drowns us in the act of love.
I wash ashore far upstream,
just below the dam,
where I lie on the fertilized lawn
and feel those angry kisses heal
like stones bleached white in the sun.

The river groans through a spillway
and shatters in foam.

The smell of water reminds me that the body

is mostly an arrogance of form,

and the kisses of strange dead women,

like cave-paintings, linger to express

the despair and exuberance

of art and flesh as they merge.

FIONA THE FEARLESS

Diane Kane

I began working at the Bristol, Massachusetts post office delivering mail in the dead of January. The ice-encrusted metal mailboxes stood on posts like sentinels of death, daring any living soul to enter. I kept a small hammer within easy reach in my mail truck to break their frozen seals. I continued my quest for months, praying for mercy from the Sun God. Little did I know what I had wished for.

The spring thaw came and turned the ice-cold containers into warm incubators for various species of creatures. The first wave of inhabitants were tiny ants. Piles of milk-white eggs formed towering pyramids inside the receptacles I thereafter referred to as bug boxes.

On any given day, I'd opened the cover to an explosion of fast-moving, minuscule specks. They poured from the hatching eggs like projectile vomit, overflowing onto the lid, across my hand, and up my arm with lightning speed. I flapped my limbs hysterically in the air, my body convulsing in jerking motions to shed them.

When the tiny ant population had birthed and dispersed, I made the acquaintance of the next wave of migrants. The bees came in all varieties, yellow jackets, hornets, and wasps. These flying devils were highly territorial. They held no regard for the mail or the government stamp on the box. They might as well have hung out a sign stating *enter at your own risk.* My allergies to bee stings of any kind took the risk to a new level. While I did carry an EpiPen with me, not getting to it in time was a constant fear. I began to open mailboxes with great trepidation.

I thought it couldn't get any worse when the next mail squatters started their invasion. My fear of spiders, although medically unfounded, was nonetheless emotionally paralyzing. Unlike bees who came with a buzzing noise and gave some warning to take cover, spiders are silent, sneaky demons. They lurked in the dark at the back of the so-called bug boxes. They build sticky webs of thick silky threads littered with the remains of their victims. To mock me, they sometimes hid crouched outside in the curved handle of the box cover, waiting for me to slip my finger around it. I'd feel the tickle of their eight oily legs rubbing together and sensed the sensation of their bodies chuckling as I screamed and pulled my hand away. I took to having to pry open the sides of the covers with my frayed fingernails to avoid this unpleasant game of hide-and-seek.

So began my education in arachnids. The various species of spiders are immense. I do believe in my delivery duties I encountered spiders who have yet to be documented by science. These spiders, undocumented and otherwise, came in multitudes of colors and varied in size and shape. Some could stretch their long-legged, thin bodies to a mere line no wider than a pencil mark, while others carried their voluptuous bodies like a crown atop thick hairy legs. They all gave me the heebie-jeebies. Then one sunny June day, I opened a box and met a spider who made me see a different side of the eight-legged creatures of my torment.

I pulled up to a particularly dilapidated mail receptacle. I marveled at the owners who kept their castle-like home and expansive yard immaculate while never giving a second thought to maintaining the box holding their mail. I was well aware that run-down boxes were an open invitation to all sorts of insects, so I performed my bug-finder ritual, which now came as second nature. I gave the outside of the box my once-over glance for any outside dwellers. Cautiously opening the lid, I paused a second to observe for any initial movement. Having cleared the first obstacles without event, I carefully leaned down to peer inside for any lurkers.

The late afternoon sun cast its waning light into the box, shining a spotlight for the dramatic entrance of the leading lady. The eight-legged damsel dashed sideways from the back of the box, turning face front when she reached the cover, claiming it as her center stage. My hand froze to the handle in petrified fear. She reared up on her four hind legs, flung out her front four legs, and expanded her body to its fullest potential. I watched in horror as her tiny jaw opened wide like a full-figured opera singer about to belt out a sonata. I was close enough to see the minuscule hairs on her black pin-top head tremble and her near enough to smell my fear. Two small beady orbs pierced me with a look of intelligence that gave me goosebumps. In case I wasn't sufficiently intimidated, she deflated, pulling her arms into her body, only to throw them out again with renewed vigor. If she were a dog, her bark would have been fierce. In fact, I had been less scared in the face of barking dogs than I was in the presence of this femme fatale. I didn't doubt she was female; after all, she was a drama queen. Our stand-off lasted for what seemed several minutes until I was able to calm my frazzled nerves.

"You are spectacular," I said. "I think I'll name you Fiona." I paused. "Fiona the Fearless." She softened her stance as though my voice put her at ease. "I have to place this mail in your box. I'll do my best not to disturb you any further."

She stepped back from the lid and moved to the side. I gently slid the letters in, taking care to lean them away from Fiona.

"You do know a yellow jacket recently occupied this box? So please take care," I said and slowly closed the cover.

Each day I arrived at Fiona's box with great anticipation. Her subsequent reaction to me mellowed with every encounter until I believe she looked forward to my visits. She would greet me with the equivalent of a wagging tail. I wished I knew her treat of preference and decided she would rather capture her own. Our conversations ranged from weather to work. We had a lot in common. She was an industrious laborer, and like me, she was subject to the whims of the elements.

One day I opened her box to find it empty of my favorite inhabitant. I noticed a white bumpy lump sitting in the corner. I'd never seen anything like it and studied it with interest. Using the edge of a letter, I touched it. My eyes widened when eight legs protruded from the bottom like the hydraulic supports of a spaceship. The white mass rose and moved slightly. Then the legs retracted, and the lump settled again.

"Fiona, is that you?" I asked. "You have quite a load there." I realized Fiona had finally confirmed my intuition that she was, in fact, a female. Dozens of tiny eggs covered her body. "Sleep well, Fiona," I whispered.

Weeks went by, and I would find Fiona's lump in different areas of the box. I was always careful not to place the mail near her. I looked beyond the box at the mini-mansion where Fiona's landlords lived. I hoped they wouldn't disturb her when they retrieved their mail.

All was going well, and I looked forward to meeting Fiona's brood. Then one day, I opened the box, and she was gone. I poked my nose inside and instantly knew I had made a horrible mistake. I heard the loud, fierce buzzing of a mad hornet. It shot out of the box and struck me in the forehead with a warning punch. I threw my arms in front of my face to fend off the next incoming launch that could hold the venom of my demise. Through the separations of my fingers, I saw Fiona race out of the box. She launched herself into the air, releasing a string of webbing behind her. I watched with amazement as she wrangled the yellow jacket in midair; her sticky line entangled the buzzing culprit. They both crashed to the ground fighting like two prize boxers. The yellow jacket didn't go down easily, but Fiona persevered. She staggered into the high grass dragging the hogtied striped villain.

"Thanks, Fiona," I called after her. I wondered where she had left her eggs. I'd have to discuss this whole episode with her tomorrow.

***

The next day, I gingerly opened the box — no, Fiona.

"Fiona," I called desperately.

I recalled the scene of the battle the day before. The angry bee buzzed with fury, twisting his body and lunging at Fiona as she methodically ensconced him in his death robe. I feared the worst. Had he hit Fiona with some of his poisonous darts in the battle? Tears filled my eyes as I waited and hoped. Through my water-distorted vision, I saw dozens of miniature versions of Fiona timidly crawling out from the darkness of the box. I wiped my eyes to clear my perception, but the multiple vision remained. The miniature Fionas reared up in unison in their show of ferocity. I smiled with pride.

"You're the spitting image of your mother," I gushed. "Fiona the Fearless would be so proud."

The tiny arachnids, one by one, dropped to all eights and parted equally to each side of the box. I tensed with fear of another bee attack when I saw a familiar body slowly approach from the shadows.

"Fiona!" I cried. "You survived."

She had the look of a battle-weary warrior who had defeated the enemy. The little ones instinctively gathered around her, and they all moved slowly to the back of the box.

"You're my hero, Fiona," I said and closed the cover quietly. I glanced at the luxurious home down the long twisting driveway. I was thankful they left their mailbox unkept and open to the creatures of nature. They would never know the superhero who lived within their midst. But I did.

CRYSTAL LAKE

Allan Fournier

I'm a '56 Chevy Belair
Station wagon in two-tone green
I belong to the Fournier Family
All in all, they're pretty keen.

I take 'em on vacation
Once a year, 'cuz for goodness sake
Work and school can get a bit stressful.
This one year, to Crystal Lake

In New Hampshire - the kids were anxious
You might say tickled pink
They say getting there's half the fun
When I'm done...let's see...what *you* think.

Mom and Dad and six kids
In my seats they all plopped down.
Then Dad, well he fired me up
And we made our way out of town.

On the highway we started to notice
My ride pretty bad - no excuse.
The mechanic had put in new shocks
But the shock nuts were all loose!

We're all human, mistakes do happen
Dad managed to hold in his ire.
He tightened them down, he buried his frown
Then soon...I got a flat tire.

At the next exit, we found a garage
Got new rubber, my wheels did sing.
But Dad, with no card for credit,
Only heard KAH-CHING!

Is anything else gonna happen?
Likely not, but... it could.
Then came the traveler's "friend," yes:
Smoke...from under...the hood

Soon the fresh mountain air had changed
Thanks to me, it really stank.
The other change Dad saw was steering
I started to drive like a tank!

The hose for my power steering
Had got nice with the manifold.
The heat burnt a hole so the fluid
The hose could no longer hold

At the next exit, we found a garage
Fluid and hose they did bring.
But Dad, with no card for credit
Only heard KAH CHING!

Finally got to the cottage,
Unpacked and soon hit the sack.
Spent a day at the lake, had some fun
The next day we…were ba…ack

On the road, that is, to visit
Some relatives on the Mom side.
We added an aunt to my seating,
I now had a lower ride.

Nine of us now, here we go
Down a road that's only two ruts
Plus a ridge down the middle, of course
Dad…would soon…go nuts.

You can guess what happened next:
Exhaust system, torn asunder.
The muffler and pipe separated
I started to sound like thunder.

A coat hanger kept 'em together,
Kinda sorta; Dad soon had headache.
On way back, we found a gas station
For repairs we hoped to make.

He didn't have parts, but took pity;
Between customers, he would weld it.
Those chunks of time, itty-bitty
And we all hoped the weld held it.

It "only" took three hours
After midnight, again on our way
We thanked our guardian angel
With a hearty vacay hurray.

One more trip to fix it up right,
No more bad news to convey.
The only thing left was the question:
How for the cottage to pay?

No plastic, the cash was gone
I'm nearing the end of this tome.
The owner knew Dad and said
"Hey, Gene…pay when…you get home"

They say getting there's half the fun.
That's the tale, in all of its glory
A pain…many ways…at the time
In the end…hey, it makes…for a story!

PARADISE FORSAKEN

Steven Michaels

That any man
Should build a dam
Seems downright deplorable;
Why should we create
A great many lakes
When divine hands have already made them?

Water is what spawned us,
So the learnéd lecterns say.
But as to why
We left the tides
Is beyond my comprehending
Perhaps it was an attempted lunge
At dangling fruits forbidden.

In reconciling Bible verse
With scientific expression,
It seems to me we were evicted
For crimes of evolution.
And fully erect
We simply left
In search of our own institutions.

With evolution came progress,

As we set about the Earth

Building and fortifying

Things of human worth.

And as in line with Eden's tale

We forsook our Mother Earth,

Who nursed us from amoeba

Then pushed us through the dirt,

Only to watch us take for granted

All that is nature's way.

Oh how awful it is to see one's offspring

Squander and betray.

Later would our ancestors

Roam the mighty desert sands.

Hoping for a Kingdom

Set down by God's own hands.

Oh they say four rivers flowed

So freely in His Eden.

It seems with each progressive step

We forgot what we were given.

So if building dams

Should lead to man's

Deplorable Damnation,

Then I think I'd rather

Surmount the sands

To seek out my salvation.

ROUTE 66

Sharon Ann Harmon

If I had ten thousand dollars

I'd go on a massively awesome

road trip, she said.

Step on the gas and wouldn't look back.

Let the wind blow onto my face,

pushing the roots of my hair

until it buckled under into the

spot in my head right under the bone.

Eat at greasy spoons, pick up hitchhikers,

sleep in rest areas and teepee motels,

and buy tacky souvenirs.

Wave at little kids in the backs of cars.

Sooth my soul with endless

miles of farmlands, industrial parks,

small towns, sea sides, honky-tonk resorts

and palatial mansions, wherever the path took me.

I'd read every billboard, count gas stations,

watch sunsets and sunrises in most every state

and see if in the end

I knew who I was.

JOURNEYS FORWARD AND BACK

Thomas Reed Willemain

Daniel Shays Highway

Reed Michael forced his attention back to the road. Any twisty, two lane road demanded attention. Route 202, past Quabbin, required even more since it threatened deer and, if the sign were to be believed, even moose.

Unfortunately, that sign started Reed thinking about moose, Maine's great killers. Then about Maine: Was he crazy to consider Lobster Land a retirement location? Nobody did that (though that was half the attraction). Then about retirement: When would his sort-of-retirement become an actual half-retirement on the way to a quarter-retirement: Zeno's Retirement? Then about whether Mother Nature would force the decision on him and push Zeno's arrow all the way home. Then about how Zeno's Paradox was actually mathematically incorrect because the infinite series did converge after all. Then about

...

Reed suddenly noticed that he'd drifted across the yellow line. Lucky this time, but next time?

His close call made Reed think about the obituaries he'd written for himself, leaving the date and cause of death as question marks in the text. That made him think about his name and all the trouble it seemed to cause other people. No, his last name wasn't

Michaels with an "s." No, his name wasn't Michael Reed. The only weirdly good thing about his quasi-backward name was that his initials in the International Phonetic Code spelled out "Romeo Mike." He chuckled as he drove: You can't get a more dudeful handle than "Romeo Mike."

Which called up memories of his old girlfriends. Number One from South Hadley began artificially. As the best friend of his best friend's girlfriend, she and Reed were pawns in somebody else's double-dating scheme. But then she turned out to be girlfriend-worthy in her own right. Until she went to UMass, joined a sorority, and her sisters turned her into a person Reed didn't recognize. Number Two appeared in his life around that time. He'd walked boldly into a dorm at Smith and asked if anybody wanted to go to a movie. That relationship lasted years too, until she left him for some Yalie. He often wondered what became of her. He was still mildly curious to know what went wrong. She'd never explained: her last words were only "Have a good life", which probably hurt worse than "drop dead" would have hurt. While Reed was licking his wounds, his buddies told him he suffered from OCS: Over-Commitment Syndrome. Apparently, that is a debilitating disease in which the victim assumes he is going to marry everybody he kisses and not the kind of thing one expects from a true man of the world.

Reed snapped back to the present. He'd unwittingly slowed down to 30 and had built up a train of frustrated followers in the ubiquitous black pickup trucks with no place to pass. So, ok, call him "Romeo Turtle." He floored it and swore to finally pay attention to the driving.

After a while his mind began to drift again, but this time forward to the actual purpose of his trip: Saying goodbye to his Uncle Ken, who was dying in hospice care at home in South Hadley. This was not daydream material, so it was eyes on the road all the way to the moment he would rather not face. On rare occasions Reed came to grips with cold reality, nailed to the here and now.

The Visit

Reed parked across the street and met the hospice nurse coming out of his uncle's house. She said yes, he was "accepting visitors" then sauntered off to her Honda. It seemed wrong that she could so quickly slip into "off duty" mode: Shut the door/shed the load. Probably a professional survival skill.

Maybe what he felt was jealousy. He dreaded this visit and worried that it would weigh on him for a long time. He had once or twice talked with people who died shortly afterwards, but those were surprises, and those folks were not family. Today was the first time Reed had walked into a conversation already knowing it to be the last. He had no game plan. He hoped to say something epic, but he knew his real ambition was merely to avoid breaking down in front of his uncle. He felt shame that his focus was his own discomfort.

Reed rang the bell. The door opened, and two strangers stared at each other. After some awkwardness, the two got it sorted out. The stranger at the door was "Uncle Reedy" from somewhere out of town. The stranger who opened the door was the daughter of a cousin from Wyoming or Idaho or someplace whom Reed probably couldn't pick out of a lineup. Once inside, Reed saw a few more familiar faces, seemingly having a grand old time catching up. That was at once reassuring and distressing—it knocked him off his vision of this as a Significant Moment in His Life. Months later, Reed would decide that the scene had been healthy and showed how much he had to learn about death and dying.

Soon it was Reed's turn to go into the bedroom to say goodbye to Uncle Ken. The once robust man who'd bravely run his LST onto exploding beaches in Italy was now skin and bones. There was no light in the eyes, and his pain was obvious in the set of his shoulders. But the soul was still in the voice, though barely a whisper, like the voice of God to Moses.

In the event, it had been almost useless to try to have a conversation of any kind. The visit reduced to one mumbled "I love you," one final kiss on the forehead, and a "goodbye." In the end, though, nothing more was needed.

OCTOBER IN KENNEBUNK

Nancy Barker Sawyer

Sandpipers play tag
with the ebbing tides.
Boardwalk stores,
once filled with tourists,
turn blank faces to the sea.
Far above the horizon,
geese call out warnings
of ominous clouds
they pass in flight.
The footprints of August
have been swept away
by nature's brisk broom.
All that remains of
Summer's sandcastles
are mounds of wet clay
and sunburned memories.

FISHERMAN AT HEAVEN'S DOOR

Phyllis Cochran

Another son has died,
Another like our own.
His time was cut too short
When God called him home.

He left us without notice,
His fish net hanging there.
The ice chest by the doorway
Made us all aware

Mike was gone too soon.
We yearned to say good-bye
His path wove through our lives,
This gentle kind of guy.

He was here the other day
This fisherman by choice.
We miss his sparkling eyes,
His joyful robust voice.

Our house, Mike's home now silent,
As painful as it is

We sought to find some comfort

In the ice chest that was his.

We now are left behind

To gather and reminisce,

Our sorrow lingers still

It's Mike we really miss.

His old green car is gone,

The ice chest was taken too.

We're left with only memories

That make us feel so blue.

God understood the ice chest.

Earthly things—our comfort here,

But where Mike fishes now

The water is crystal clear.

With hope we look to the lakes

Watch ripples lapping the shore.

By faith we can see Mike

Fishing by Heaven's door.

Yes, another son has died -

Another like our own -

We'll see him again one day

When God calls us home.

THESE ARE THOSE RUSSET LEAVES THAT CLING

Dee Matthews

...these are those russet leaves that cling

—Edna St. Vincent Millay

and cling

before the last

hold released

to rise first

on a small

current of wind

hope beyond hope

aloft adrift

then swirl

then twist

then rush

to the fall

to the end

to the earth

THE ESCAPE

Maggie Nerz Iribarne

Summers in Salem were busy. Although the students from the state university had dispersed in May the town was crowded, full of tourists wanting to get their auras measured and buy cheap trinkets at the junk stores. But Cecilia almost always stayed home. Her mother insisted.

The wind chimes tinkled, summoning Cecilia from her thoughts, leading her to the doorway, enticing her to put a cool hand on the knob, turn the lock, open the door, step outside. The heat, conflicting sharply with their overly air-conditioned house, felt like a slap.

Why would you want to be outside with all those thieves and murderers? Ma's voice played on and on inside Cecilia's head.

Cecilia's feet were bare on the dry grass as she listened to the hum of a distant lawn mower, a sound she enjoyed, remembering Daddy mowing every Saturday. Now an old man with a pot belly came to do it, and when he did, Ma closed all the blinds and double bolted the doors.

A rustling sound caused Cecilia to move to the side yard and survey a long row of hedges, a well-groomed series of bushes she never noticed. She stared, struggling and failing to remember Daddy clipping these pristine plants. Then, another movement made Cecilia's heart beat in her chest and her body almost turned to run. *Ma was right. Murderers and thieves.* The bushes continued to shake until a swathe of green opened to allow the exit of the fattest orange tabby cat Cecilia had ever seen. It sidled out, looking confident and purposeful, and walked straight to Cecilia, who leaned down to touch its velvety coat. It brushed with all its might against Cecilia's legs, causing a warm rush. A heart-shaped tag hung from the cat's neck: Bishop.

"Hello, Bishop," Cecilia's long black braid hung down as she rubbed the purring neck. The cat lumbered back to the bushes, which opened again to reveal a passageway. He turned for a fast peek back at Cecilia, seeming to say *follow me* just by a glance. Cecilia looked back at the house and down at her bare feet, knowing she left the door unlocked behind her, and followed the cat into the hedge.

On the other side was a creamy yellow house with white trim and ivy and roses growing over the front. The cat padded up the front steps and into the cat flap while Cecilia froze in her tracks. *What am I doing?* She was about to get down on all fours and try to squeeze into the cat's entrance.

"Well! Look what the cat dragged in!" An old lady with blood red hair, a psychedelic green floral print housecoat, and large black glasses appeared at the door. She reached in her pocket to pull out some ravaged tissues and blew her nose with a honk.

"Well, you finally made it, girlie!"

Cecilia smiled a little, then frowned at the over-familiarity.

"The cat," Cecilia said.

"Yes, that's the Bishop. You know I've often thought you're too old and I'm too young to be stuck inside all summer. We've got something in common!" Cecilia stood frozen. "Come in! Come in! I'd love a chat. " Cecilia turned to look for her own home. *Ma would be there soon.* "Oh, don't worry girlie, she's not even close." Cecilia's eyes focused on the old lady's kind expression, and she could not help but step through the door.

"My George died and nothing's the same. He kept me feeling free. Now I feel a little cooped up. I told you we have things in common! Glad the Bishop's here. He just turned up! Just like you. Can you imagine?" Cecilia followed the old lady silently down a hallway to the kitchen. All the way, the Bishop trotted alongside them.

The old lady's house, hot as Cecilia's was cold, felt comfortable, like being in a sleeping bag. The woman picked up a sweaty milk carton from the table and poured some of its contents into a chipped pink flowered teacup. "Here you go, my prince," she said to the Bishop, setting the cup in front of the cat.

"Ah!" the old lady said. "Now for your tea."

They entered a long dining room with a peach glow and an earthy smell. From a corner china cabinet crammed with mismatched pottery the old lady extricated a crystal decanter. She turned to a sideboard where four wine glasses sat on a tarnished tray. "A little dusty," she said, lifting and eyeing the glasses with scrutiny, pulling her housecoat by its hem and wiping out their insides. Cecilia knew her Ma—though she, herself, rarely cleaned—would not have approved of this method. *Gross*, is what Ma would say.

A wave of irritation momentarily consumed Cecilia. She needed to stop thinking about Ma. *Enjoy this.* With that intention she felt lighter, empty of her burden.

The old lady removed the crystal stopper from the decanter, and poured the ruby red tea into the glasses. Cecilia would remember that depth of color forever.

"That's right, you make up your mind and there's no telling what can happen," the old lady said.

Next, she led Cecilia into her living room where, like her china cabinet, mismatched furniture pieces crowded the space. Books wallpapered every wall , and a bay window loomed out onto an open field. Cecilia did not recognize the view and could not figure out which way the old lady's house was turned to face such a space. A small yellow bird hopped around in a cage.

"That's Jorge," the old lady said, "Now sit, girlie, drink your tea slow. Enjoy this." She handed Cecilia a glass, and left the room.

When the old lady returned, she carried with her a plate of sliced pear. "Endicotts. Oldest fruit tree in the country." She moved to a side table, picked up a nearby box of matches, struck up a flame, and lit a single yellow taper candle in a silver holder. Cecilia enjoyed the familiar smell of sulfur while her host settled back in worn cushions with a slight groan. "Sometimes I fall asleep like this," she grunted, then out-and-out cackled, holding her glass in her cupped hand. "That's why everything is stained!" She burst out in laughter again, smacking her lips and studying her guest.

Cecilia enjoyed the strange combination of tea and pear mingled in her mouth. She put her head back, and relaxed into the swirling effect of this strange, surprising house. She knew the old lady was talking, and she was talking back, but it all seemed effortless and easy.

"You okay over there, with your Ma, girlie?" the old lady asked.

"What? Yes, of course," *Ma.* Cecilia snapped alert.

The old lady's eyes softened, her head tilted in sympathy.

Dark thoughts about Ma came rushing back, like a punch in the stomach. She'd arrive home, search for Cecilia, go ballistic. *She could not stay here. She would have to go back.*

"I guess I should go. Ma will wonder-" Cecilia stood abruptly, knocking her glass to the floor. Flustered, she offered the old lady a hasty apology, then rushed past her to the doorway where the Bishop was licking his milky chops.

The old lady stood with some effort, leaned on her floral cane, and smiled a toothless grin. "I'll be here for you when you're ready." |

Ready for what?

Cecilia sped back to the hedge, worried she would not find it, but as she approached the area, or what she thought might be the area, there it was, leading to her own stifling backyard.

Inside, she found her house extra quiet, with just the hum of the refrigerator and air conditioner. She looked at the clock: 10:15. Ma usually left at 10 AM and came back at noon. *Strange. Hadn't I been gone for hours?*

The air conditioning sent an unnatural chill through her body. She grabbed a book, and moved out the side door again, pretending to wait for Ma. She sat on a chaise lounge and watched, hoping to see the Bishop's orange body meandering back again across the hedge. But this was impossible, for when she looked, there was no hedge, only a rickety fence and empty lot on the other side. Overtaken by exhaustion, Cecilia lay back on the chair, and despite the extreme heat, she fell asleep.

In what seemed like a minute, Ma's wide shadow jolted Cecilia awake. Ma stood aghast, eyes narrowed in accusation.

"What are you doing out here?" she said, out of breath.

"Just reading, and sleeping," Cecilia said, sitting up.

"Out here?" Ma said.

"I have a headache," Cecilia diverted, "I should probably get some aspirin."

Ma's face brightened and distracted her from any suspicions she might have been forming. She loved illness, especially Cecilia's.

"Oh, honey, go to the cupboard and get some now. I could use some too. Twisted my ankle on one of those darn cobblestones downtown."

Cecilia hurried inside with Ma limping at her heels.

They ate lunch together from matching TV trays, a courtroom show turned up too loud. Cecilia realized she could not feel or taste one trace of the warm sensation the old lady's tea and pears gave. The chill of the freezing house and greasy taste of burgers had taken over all her senses.

***

Tracy appeared out of nowhere the fall after the summer of the old lady encounter. Moving from class to class, Cecilia, now a senior in high school, kept seeing the same girl again and again. If she went to the restroom, the girl would be leaving. If she waited in line in the cafeteria, the girl waited in the same line. One day, she found out the girl's name: Tracy.

Cecilia knew the rumors about Tracy. Ma told her. "That poor girl's father chased her and her mother across the golf course with an axe. Terrible. And they were wealthy, too. All the snooty folks turned their backs on them." Ma chuckled gently to herself. Ma loved when she could talk about the snooty folks.

Before she met Tracy, Cecilia suspected what Ma said was true, that all the other kids were snoots or snobs or bullies or ignoramuses, that Cecilia should stay away from them all. But Tracy broke Ma's spell of negativity by being kind and gentle and fun and easy to be around. For the first time since Daddy died, Cecilia felt a little joy. They joked about their teachers, like Mr. Wooton, the incredibly dorky but well-meaning French teacher, they speculated about the size of Mrs. Sank's panty hose (Double Huge), and they protected each other from flying balls "mistakenly" chucked at them during gym.

"Is it true your mom is, um, afraid of everything?" Tracy asked one day over Salisbury steaks in the cafeteria.

"Um, I'm not sure, kind of, I guess," Cecilia's fork dragged through grey gravy.

"Is it true she's crazy? That she treats you bad?" Tracy's wide eyes stared.

"Well is it true about your dad?" Cecilia erupted in defense.

"I actually didn't know I was abused until he tried to kill me and my mom, even though he'd been pulling stuff for years. I had no idea. It was weird," she paused, "Do you know?"

"Know what?" Cecilia said.

"That you're abused?"

Cecilia thought about that. She considered her Daddy, *Daddy* was abused. Ma could be so mean, especially to him. "Corey, look at this wimpy guy," she'd wag a plump finger at the screen, "He reminds me of you." She'd laugh and laugh, and strangely, Daddy would too.

For Cecilia, she knew she wasn't abused like Daddy, and it wasn't physical.. It was just that Ma wanted everything, she wanted to fill their house and Cecilia with all of her own problems and sadness and fears and desires, with no room for anything else.

That day, Cecilia accepted that she, like Tracy, was abused. Having bonded over that status, the two girls always found each other in class or in the lunchroom.They didn't need to get into every detail of their stories, instead, the new friends had an unspoken promise to pretend to be normal.

But then the year ended, and Tracy announced she and her mother were moving to an aunt's in Texas.

"Well, maybe I can visit," Cecilia said, looking past Tracy's shoulder, avoiding her friend's truthful eyes.

"I'll write every week! Real letters. Super old fashioned. It's not like we have anything better to do," Tracy said in a burst of false brightness.

They both knew Ma would intercept the letters. And they both knew if they traded emails, Ma, who demanded to know Cecilia's passwords, would read them. Cecilia hoped Tracy would have a better life, and dreamed someday that she could move somewhere, too.

***

"Ma, do you know any of our neighbors?" Cecilia asked one night. The two of them were deeply invested in a new show called *Love without Sight*, where couples become engaged without ever seeing each other. Ma thought this was a brilliant idea, like magic. "I don't know what I saw in your father. You would've thought I was blind," she laughed. Cecilia eyed her mother with contempt, a feeling bubbling up more often.

"But have you ever met any of our neighbors?" Cecilia repeated.

"Huh? Of course not," Ma said, staring at the screen, shoving popcorn in her wide open mouth. "Neighbors are nosy."

***

Finally, on her 18th birthday, Cecilia asked Ma if she could get them both a sandwich from the new fast food joint on the far side of town. Ma smiled faintly, for she had made no secret her desire to try the Chickie Burger Supreme. "What a good girl, you are, Cecilia, always thinking of your Ma." Cecilia snuggled up against her and kissed her odorless white cheek. Ma stiffened a little, unused to this affection.

As soon as Ma pulled out of the driveway, Cecilia jumped up, and moved out the back door. She made sure her feet were bare again, that she planted herself on the same patch of dry grass as before, waiting, waiting. She squeezed her eyelids shut, cramped her fists into balls, and conjured every spirit she could, asking Daddy, Tracy, and of course the old lady, to help her, to save her. Everyone in the neighborhood was at work, everyone was always somewhere, except her. Long repressed tears ran down her cheeks.

After what felt like hours, with the weight of her exhaustion and self-pity almost too much to bear, Cecilia opened her eyes to see that the perfect hedge had appeared, the passageway had opened, and the Bishop had emerged, his nose sniffing, tail straight up in the air. Cecilia held out her hand, and squatted. When she straightened herself, the old lady stood at the entrance of the path, leaning on her flowered cane.

"There you are, girlie, we've been waiting for you. How've you been?" The old lady looked exactly the same, even the same housecoat, her bright smile like a force field begging Cecilia's face to brighten, too.

"Not too good," Cecilia admitted, approaching the old lady without hesitation, folding herself into outstretched arms, sobbing and resting her head on the soft, lavender scented shoulder. Holding Cecilia, she repeated, "There, there, girlie, there there, Bridget understands, Don't we Bishop, don't we?" He wound around their ankles.

"Now, let's go over to my place and have a nice glass of tea. Would you like that?"

Cecilia wiped her eyes.

Bridget. Her name is Bridget.

"Yes, yes, I'd like that, Bridget, " said Cecilia, so glad to know her name, to finally know her name.

"Are you ready to go?" the old lady asked, taking Cecilia's hand in hers.

"Yes, I'm ready," she said, sniffling.

"Good. Good girl. Let's go then," the old lady said. "Come, Bishop."

They approached the open hedge, stepping through to Bridget's yard, the bushes closing behind them for good.

END

LONG AND SHORT OF IT

Michael Young

Farmyard split rail fence
impedes the path to
rustic barn,
doors open,
sheltered beneath an oak.
The challenge,
a choice -
whether to fence-lean,
take in the lilac scented
long view or
find the gate.
Goodness knows what
ancient treasures
may lurk
Inside the shadowy
barn bays.
The smell of
old leather harness -
the rough finish of
wrought iron hardware -
the faded sweetness of
leftover hay.
Who's to say
I have to choose on
this bright, vacation day?
Better have both -
one, then the
other.

ODE TO LAKE MATTAWA

Karen Traub

Bald eagles are back from the brink of extinction
Angling for bass, enjoying the morning
Like the guy casting from shore who just might be thinking
"A bad day of fishing beats a good day of working"

Wisps of mist like ghosts in a hurry
Reveal silent kayakers in orange vests at dawn
Hank, the great blue heron, swoops in and lands on ballerina legs
The water's so clear you can see the skeleton trees fifteen feet down

Mattawa; where the waters meet
Dammed for pleasure over a hundred years ago
While big brother Quabbin over the hill
Drowned four towns to quench Boston's thirst

Blueberry island has plenty for kids and cardinals
A rabbit will size you up, then bunny hop away
Chipmunks like spies, peer and dart among the rocks and crevices
The circus squirrels trapeze from tree to tree

Marlboro butts and Fireball nips
The squawking cries of Mrs. mallard tangled in a nest of line

Rubber worms fall off hooks, grow and explode in toxic waste

Coke cans, golf balls, cinder blocks, a toddler's sneaker left behind

The plop of a frog startled off a log

A pair of loons silhouetted in the afternoon

Hummingbirds mating and fighting

The rattle cry of the belted kingfisher on a mission

Roiling swirls of crappies ripple across the water like a serpent

A Baltimore Oriole's flash of orange in green trees

Parachutes from a small plane pop open to decorate the sky

Fork-tailed swallows give way to evening bats

A playground and ecosystem

Nature in balance

To be shared and cherished

By fish, fowl, and human

PATHWAYS OF THE SOUL

Memoir, Grief, and Loss Writing

THE CHRISTMAS BOX

Cathy Carlton Hews

I saw it from the top of the stairs. A very big box nestled against the bottom step. I paused and looked at it. They had told me it was coming. "Oh, we sent you something, it's something in a box but shoot it won't get there for Christmas. But be on the lookout for a box."

No, this probably isn't it. This box is BIG. They didn't say, "be on the lookout for a BIG box." They said "be on the lookout for a box." So I'm figuring, oh yeah, cool, a box of fudge. A box of notecards (hey, write us more, you loser cousin, you) a box of playing cards, a box of hair, a box of anything. A small box of anything.

I look down the stairs again. The big box is still there. I see no Amazon logos, insignia. Oh huh. Somebody sent somebody in this building a box of something they packed themselves. How nice.

I venture down the first step and slowly, head down, totter down a few more. I study the carpet. It's a pretty blue-gray with yellow and pink flecks. It's always spotlessly clean. I wonder how my building management keeps it so pristine. I never see work people in the hall. I wonder about that for a minute or two, on the fourth step from the bottom.

On the third step from the bottom I rev it up. I leap past the box out the front door, not looking at the addressee. Think about looking at the addressee later.

My brother and I were very young children on the one Christmas we had as kids. The morning was a bright, cold day in northern Maine. Icicles were on the trees outside. The sun was shining and the snow on the windows sparkled like diamonds. Those diamonds rode in on the sunbeams that Christmas morning. My parents were both there, my mother was normal and we opened presents under the tree. I'm sure we had more than one each, my brother and I, but it became a face-off between the two "big" gifts, last to be opened.

I opened mine, a big wrapped thing with a fine, proud red bow, and thus was born Twinky! The teddy bear was almost as big as me, and Twinky also sported a fine, proud, red bow. Twinky would be my confidante, traveling companion and secret-holder for many years to come. Larry watched and clapped. He then opened his, which was very oddly wrapped. Snowshoes. He looked at the snowshoes, our parents beaming at the holiday sight. Then Larry let out the biggest howl of sorrow, probably heard up in Canada that day. He cried for all the teddy bear-less Christmases past and future. He howled all the diamonds out of the sunbeams. He, inconsolable, would not stop crying. The snowshoes might as well have been the Pink Bunny Suit. My mother, shocked, giggled a bit and murmured, "well, Larry." I do believe I offered to let him hold Twinkie for a bit, but not for long, little Christmas bitch that I was. There was nothing more satisfying than winning at Christmas, especially over a pesty little brother.

Larry and I would meet up at Christmas again, a few years down the road.

I come back from errands and open the front door. The box is still there. I walk up to it and look down at the label. Yes, it's for me. I don't recognize the return label, but I know it is from my adored

Philadelphia cousins, the only family I have left. Leaving the box there, I keep walking up the stairs.

Next day, I bring the box upstairs. It's big, unwieldy. I drag it up, one pretty blue-gray with yellow and pink flecks carpeted step at a time. I open my apartment door, swatting back the ever-escaping Cheddar the cat, (you're gonna get a switch in your stocking, little mister) and push the box inside. I move the box to one corner of the room. I leave it there. I leave it there for another day.

My friend had left a few days earlier to spend the holidays with his kids and little grandson. Christmas Day he had sent me a picture of his grandson aboard his new toy tractor. Wow! So cute! How happy that kid looked with his tractor. I kept looking at that picture. The tractor was definitely a Twinky gift, not snowshoes. I thought of my brother.

After the Twinky Christmas, we never celebrated the holiday again. My mother went downhill fast, lost in alcohol and madness. And religion.

The year we moved to western Massachusetts, I was in fifth grade and starting to push back against the insanity. She had gotten involved with the Jehovah's Witnesses, something I could never join in on. No birthdays, no holidays, etc... She was as intense about them as she was about alcohol. She forgot she had kids, which was just fine by me. My father was absent, so it was Larry and me looking out for each other.

That first Christmas, Larry (and me, truth be told) was upset that we didn't have a Christmas tree. This was a peer pressure thing, boy, all the classmates want to know if your tree is up. I took him upstairs and we managed to scrounge up some ribbons and bows and colored construction paper and we decorated the coat rack that was on the second floor. YES, our tree was up! Now we could say that, too. One afternoon my mother came across our tree and asked about it. I told her our tree was up, now, too and trotted downstairs. I glanced back. She stood there a long time, looking at the tree.

I dragged the box over to the couch. It was time. I opened it and immediately started to cry. It was filled to the brim with all kinds of wrapped things, with bows, and candy canes taped to everything. (Oh my God, I'm going to get a tractor!) A Christmas stocking! I have never had a Christmas stocking in my life. Nail polish, bath bombs, hair ties, socks, a wonderfully soft throw blanket, and holiday tissues. And cat toys! A cat Christmas ornament. A zester that I had been longing for on Facebook. Somebody was paying attention on Facebook, I realized and cried even harder. My sweet niece, M, I suspect. All those ordinary things that families do. I texted my out of town friend and asked him, "Is this what normal people do?" Yes, Cathy, that's pretty much what "normal" people do. He did have the good grace to set off "normal," which I was grateful for.

One of my cousins had made a wooden Santa some years back. It had belonged to my aunt, recently departed. They said for me to have it. They also gave me a beautiful cross ornament of hers. My father had a crocheted cloth cross by him. I came across it one day when I was making him dinner.

"Daddy, where did this come from?" I asked him.

Neither of us were likely to have a cross. He said he didn't know. I took it away, but soon put it back near him on his table. I suppose a caretaker left it there, but I never solved that mystery. It went with him to the nursing home, it was with us the day he died. I had kept it, somewhere here in a drawer. I pulled it out and saw it was a little worse for the wear, dirty and tattered.

I hung it on my little tree with my Aunt's cross.

What normal people do, I guess.

NATALIE MERING

Aidan Needle

Mom who gave me her
milk on a planet burning
don't let your love melt away
and let me lay in your bed.

It's cold and icy at night;
and I need you to hold me close
under your comforter; to sing me a
lullaby as the outside rooms turn to ash.

When I'm ready to leave your nursery,
painted in dark blues and maroons,
send me down the road with a tune
and your palm-print warmed with your kiss warm, on my ungrateful
cheek.

The truth is I never had a mother
to come home to in the summer, so
let me visit you in the California swelter, when
you're dancing and strumming beyond the pathways

And take me out for coffee and an

open mic where I beg you to sing

70s psych rock with me. As the last slide guitar

plays us out, look me in the eyes and say you love me.

Like Miriam,

lead me through a rising tide and

tell me all the stories of your childhood

how much you want me to be better

How much you wanted to be better.

As past leaves,

and future comes,

I'll remember the day I first heard your voice

the joy you had as you welcomed me to this world.

A WALK THROUGH LIFE

Jeanne D. Gilbert

At a distance someone was approaching on foot. I hesitated from hauling the water buckets from the truck into the field where four Shetland ponies enjoyed the grass. The man dragged his foot along the macadam with both arms in a fixed position. Was he on drugs or drunk? I couldn't tell by the way he moved his body. My body tensed and went into flight mode.

Closer and closer came the figure. As he approached, the smile on his face eased my anxiety.

"Hi. Are those your ponies?" he asked.

"Yes. This is Dream. This is Cinnamon Swirl. They were born on the farm. This one is Satin and the shy one is Beauty. They are sisters."

From that moment our friendship began, one step at a time.

Jerry would stop by my farm occasionally to visit, mainly to say hello to the horses and to extend his deformed arms to scratch their necks. He often enjoyed the glass of refreshing apple cider I offered. Once he explained that in the course of a week he would travel on foot for miles on end. He couldn't keep track of how often he needed a new pair of shoes to replace his worn-out ones. The distance between the house where he lived with his parents and the farm consisted of traveling through two towns.

Unfortunately, not everyone showed Jerry an understanding

heart. Three miles away at another farm the owners told him not to stop and visit their horses in the fields. They claimed that the apples Jerry gave to their horses made the horses sick. He wasn't even allowed to scratch their necks.

I'm not sure how and when Jerry's path in life changed. We never discussed our personal lives. But as an adult he eagerly offered to help pastors and ministers perform their duties for their congregations, even with his physical limitations. His repertoire of fascinating stories had no end.

On a cold December evening, my husband, a friend, and I attended a Christmas service in a country church. We had the pleasure of spending time with Jerry while enjoying refreshments in the basement. A voice inside me said, "Offer to give Jerry a ride home." Another voice inside me said, "You've had an extremely busy day and driving to Jerry's house is out of the way." The debate went on for a few minutes. Finally I decided to ask Jerry, "Do you have a ride home? We can take you."

He smiled and happily accepted my offer.

In the news the following night we learned that Jerry had been hit by a car crossing a busy intersection that morning—that same intersection he would have crossed the night we took him home. He was rushed to the hospital. He died the next day.

THE OLD OAK

Jessica Vincent

The river ran cold and swiftly,
Its waters blackish blue.
Into its depths her thoughts were drifting
Straining for sanctity anew.

Rotting branches of the bank-side oak.
Ancient remnants of a once-dry field,
Flooded by the dams of man, they did soak
In the heaviest rains and the river's yield.

Pensively she sat, the heavens had cleared.
But the storms that cloud her heart remained.
The love-loss ache she had always feared,
Reflected by the river; she saw her self-disdain.

She dipped her hands in slowly,
The icy sting moved up her arm.
To squelch her sickened heartbeat only.
She had not intended to cause herself harm.

But the angry oak began to moan
A pitiful cry of its former glory.

The shifting creaks of its dying form
Raised to her mind her own sad story.

She began to weep behind the tree,
And stroked its bark with her frozen fingers.
In its molded texture she could see
Her own illness; the pain that lingers.

To expire beneath it would take too long,
Though its ignoble death she wished to share.
Her broken heart was still beating strong,
Yet with will to live it did not pair.

The current's gentle rhythm allayed her fear
Of the mortal plunge she opted to take.
How wide her eyes became when she did peer
Into Death's own, if only for pity's sake.

With the constancy of the pain becoming old
She felt in her soul already dead.
So she lunged forth, bracing for the cold
The frame of her body, solid as lead.

Beneath the angry branches swaying,
Into the frigid water she dropped.
But her soul, with the oak, forever shall stay

To dwell eternally, though her heart had stopped.

Together now they muse under the stars,

Beside the river's permanent flow.

This tale of the girl and the oak could be ours,

If we listen to whispering trees we don't know.

WHERE THERE IS LOVE...

Sue Moreines

I'd never been to a wake before, until today. My parents made me stand next to them in the receiving line for two hours as one person after another stopped, shook my hand, and said how sorry they were. I didn't want to "receive" their condolences, or anything else for that matter. I just wanted to run away, as fast and as far as I could.

When the torture was finally over, I was allowed to escape to the silence of my room. I laid down on the bed, closed my eyes, and wondered: *Is this what it felt like Jacob? You were laying on a silky white sheet, your head cradled by a fluffy pillow, your hands stretched out beside you. Everyone said you were very handsome, and looked like you were sleeping. Mom bought you a new shirt and pants for the terrible occasion, and your hair was combed exactly like mine. Although your lips were thin and closed, I visualized your smile, the one that only we could share.*

Burying my face deep into the comforter, I sobbed for the longest time while replaying the horrifying accident. When I was able to sit up I looked over at Jacob's empty bed, and again became overwhelmed by grief. My head exploded with questions: *How am I ever going to get through this? Why? Why did he have to fall? Wasn't there something I could have done to help him? Will Jacob ever forgive me?*

Grabbing a pen and a notebook from my desk, I sat down at the foot of his bed and decided to write him a letter:

Dear Jacob,

I swear I never meant to hurt you. It was an accident! We've hiked around that gorge hundreds of times and neither of us ever got so much as a scratch. I hate thinking about the second you tripped over my hiking boot and flew headfirst over the ledge. If not for the lone tree growing horizontally out of the rocks, you would have sailed to the very bottom. A branch pressed against your chest and dropped you into a crevice a few feet below. I had to leave you, Jacob. I had to get help. I'm so sorry I couldn't climb down to save you. You can't begin to imagine how sorry I am. I'm sorry for me too. Why did you have to trip Jacob? Why did you have to leave me?

I never really believed in heaven, until I saw your lifeless body placed gently on a stretcher and loaded into the ambulance. At that very moment, I knew you were on your way to Paradise. Then I collapsed onto the hot sand, getting as close to Hell as I possibly could.

Someone picked me up and put me

into the back of a police car. I think people were talking to me since I saw their mouths moving, but I didn't hear anything. All I did was stare at my reflection in the Plexiglass divider. I wanted to believe you were alive and sitting there, right across from me.

I remember when Casey died. We walked down to the creek and hurled stones into the water until our arms ached. You said, Casey crossed the Rainbow Bridge and would patiently wait until we could see her again. If that's really true, she's leaning up against you now, as you stroke her head and scratch behind her ears.

I know my life won't be the same without you Jacob, and I feel so afraid and alone. I thought the bond we shared for 16 years was strong and unbreakable, but now it's shattered, and the most important part of me is gone.

The love I feel for you has only grown stronger, and nothing will ever change that.

Your other half,

Max

I put the letter into an envelope, and as silly as it may sound, I attached a Forever stamp and addressed it to:

Jacob Hart

Somewhere in Heaven

I changed my clothes, laced up my hiking boots, put the envelope in my back pocket and headed out the door. My parents hollered for me to come back, but I was on a mission and would deal with the consequences later.

I retraced our steps heading back to the gorge and stood at the exact spot where I held my breath and Jacob's was taken seconds later. The sand was still hot and the tree remained tightly secured by its deep roots. What I said aloud was personal, meant only for my brother and for me. When I finished, I held up the letter and a gust of wind lifted it from my hand and guided it across the valley and out of sight.

After our hikes, Jacob and I always went into town for ice cream. I was halfway there before I even realized it. I suppose it's true…old habits never die.

To my surprise, there was no line at the ice cream shop. I ordered the usual, two chocolate/vanilla twist cones with rainbow sprinkles. Holding one in each hand, I sat down on our favorite bench to indulge, people watch, and enjoy a sweet memory.

***

After eating, Jacob and I made sure to check out the new books and magazines in the book store window. Today wasn't going to be any different. However, as I approached, I could see there wasn't a single thing on display. But I did notice someone who looked exactly like me, staring out through the glass. When we made direct eye contact a feeling of warmth flowed through my body. I felt energized and calm at the exact same time. In his left hand, he held Casey's collar and with his right, gave a thumb's up as if to say, everything is fine, no need to worry. We smiled, in mirror image, and I felt whole again. Moments later, the lights above him flickered, and he was gone. In his place was a new book titled,

"Where There is Love, No One Ever Dies"

GRIEF

Nancy Barker Sawyer

I comfort your brother
  as he mourns for you.
I comfort your brother,
  that's what mothers do.
We weep together
  as we hold one another.
I see your face
  in the face of your brother.
Broken and bruised
  we go on, as we must.
But the joy has gone
  and most of the trust.
Memories flood us
  as we try to go on.
Your laughter, your kindness
  from the day you were born.
But your brother is brave,
  memoires without you have begun.
Where there were just you two
  now there is one.
I comfort your brother
  as he mourns for you.

I comfort your brother,

that's what mothers do.

NEW ORPHAN'S FIRST STEPS

Gerard Sarnat

"The only thing that makes life possible
is permanent, intolerable uncertainty:
not knowing what comes next."

—Ursula K. Le Guin, *The Left Hand of Darkness*

Back top shelf bedroom closet

of long-deceased Doctor Sarnat,

his son & granddaughter —also

left-handed but still ticking MDs

rummaging balanced on a ladder

among sealed boxes, soiled bandages

amid bladder catheters circa Eisenhower,

uncover then instinctively almost toss

in our necessarily growing junk pile

next to donation stacks or (long-shot)

estate sale worthies of accumulation

—disposition must precede sprucing up,

putting their condominium on the market

one nondescript dense black plastic sack appears

holding some missing silver: the family jewels.

IS IT THE DOG'S BIRTHDAY?

Cathy Carlton Hews

I should get up at some point. Memorial Day Weekend. Three days of unstructured time. I used to look forward to that.

Why does that cat box stink like a motherfucker? That new litter blows. It was lightweight, that new light kind. That's why you bought it. You were at the Big Y, just out from visiting the nursing home.

I forced myself to shop that day.

It's hot, I can barely push the cart. I should call the physical therapist, any physical therapist. It's not helping you are still reeling from that car accident. Well, reeling is perhaps overstating it, but it's painful, even more painful than usual to stand for five minutes.

OK, so we are running out of gas just pushing the shopping cart. The litter is on the other end of the store. Fuck.

Stand in the deli line for crab cakes? No, I don't care anymore, grab fish sticks on the way past frozen foods.

What do I have at home? I have a big jug of Pinot in the fridge. Yeah, fish sticks and Pinot. That's all I can manage anyway. I can cancel the rest of this and just barely make it to the checkout line. I am starting to sweat and shake. It's all been a bit much for one day, no?

Dad didn't look so good today, that weird thing is growing on his back. I'm going to have to talk to a doctor about that.

God it's hot in here. I could use a nap. I wonder if I curled up next to the kidney beans anybody would notice. Maybe I don't have to go all the way to the cat litter aisle, maybe not. FUCK, they're out of food, too. That's right. I can slide on the litter another day or so, but somehow those two furry freaks are insistent upon eating. Alright, we can do it. If I position most of my upper body over the cart, I can roll myself to the other end, push off with one foot. Roll me away. I roll up the pet aisle, panting like a sheepdog locked inside a Toyota in July. I realize I am more fucked than a bagful of kittens headed to the lake.

Rolling past toilet paper (fuck do I need toilet paper, fuck it I don't care, I have paper towels still, I think) I hit the pet aisle. Grab a few cans of Friskies wet pâté, not shredded, and I eye cat litter. I might as well, I'm here. I am really feeling ill in the heat, though. You can't carry this heavy stuff, no way. Though the load is lightened with all the things you didn't buy as you bargained your way out of this shopping trip. Good call on the fish sticks, way lighter than crab cakes. I know I won't be able to hoist the heavy litter into the cart. Then I spy it. 50% lighter! Lightweight biodegradable container! A variety of fragrances: Cherry Apple Orchard, Lilac Rose Garden, Vanilla Cinnamon Buddha Pie. 50% Lighter! As I feel myself slipping down the cart I grab the lightweight litter and toss it, almost effortlessly, in the cart.

Weeping with relief, I head to the checkout. The lady looks at me kindly as I hang on to the little electronic payer-thing, swiping the first card I could grab. Sweating, swallowing down bile, I make idle chitchat, as human beings do. (Please don't notice that I am collapsing, please don't notice my weird breathing, please don't notice that I am alone here in this part of the country I never wanted to be back in for a second taking care of someone who never had a chance in hell himself, who never made a sacrifice for me yet I am sacrificing everything, my friends, my art, my way of life, please don't notice any of this.)

"Pretty hot today, huh?" I chirp, as I (artfully, or so it seems to me) switch my death-clutch from the electronic payer-thing back to the cart as to avoid fainting outright.

"Wow, I should make those two little furry boys get jobs, huh?" as the pâté and NEW! Lightweight Apple Orchard roll through, maybe totaling twelve bucks. The cashier looks at me, laughs nervously, and looks around.

"Oh yes," she says. Someone has joined her, as if an invisible Cashier Bat Signal has gone up. The second cashier starts to bag, eyes me, says cheerily,

"Wow, sure is hot." Eyes me again. "Will you need help out to your car, ma'am?"

What day is it? Saturday? Oh yes, Saturday, Sunday, Monday. Great three days. I have three days to change the litter. Drag a mop over these floors, go see Pops in the Shady Rest. You have to write, you have to exercise, you have to figure out doctor appointments. You have to nap.

I wake up. Noon. Christ. Get up, you have to get up.

I put coffee on. I stumble back to the couch. Why the hell does that litter stink so much? It's the new litter I bought this week, that's what it is. NEW! 50% lighter! Apple Orchard Fresh. It smells like a cat shit in the orchard. Yeah, I got to change that box today, add that to the list, I'll do that. What time is it, noon? I flick on the TV. Damn, I missed all the Saturday Good Eats episodes. Now I am stuck with that stupid pioneer woman with her redneck-husband-on-the-ranch-bullshit. I hate-watch that for a while. What time is it now? Close enough to whatever time I need it to be. I pour some wine. Hey, it's the weekend, I have three days ahead to do all that stuff. I heat something up in the microwave. I pour some more wine.

I think about going to see Dad. No, there's two more days for that. I slip in a Tony Shalhoub Monk DVD. I watch two episodes. I eat something else. I cry over the one where Mr. Monk has to give back the kid he is fostering 'cause Mr. Monk can't take care of him. It's so unfair that Mr. Monk can't have that kid, why can't he have that little piece of happiness? But, no, Mr. Monk can't take care of the kid, I know it's the right thing to do, I know in my heart of hearts Mr. Monk can't take care of that kid. The new family the kid gets looks alright, I guess. I cry some more anyway. I watch two more. Two easier ones, ones where Randy fucks something up or something. Easy. I walk past the cat box, closing my eyes and holding my breath. Yes, I will do that today, yes, I will.

I think about my father. Maybe I will see him tomorrow. Maybe I won't. I don't want to go today. Maybe I will go tomorrow.

Too many things happened at the same time: the Alzheimer's finally becoming too terrifying to be safe, this opportunity to change over to work at the college where I want to be, the house flipped over into my name, oops, only a year contract at the college, that's OK, sign, sign, sign, it will take you a year to unload this hellhole anyway. I'll go tomorrow. What time is it now?

I land back on the couch. Can I do another Monk? One more to calm me, one more to put out the fire.

I do that. I choke on cat litter fumes. I drink more wine. I don't write. I feed the cats their dinner though I don't think it's their dinner time.

I think I need to go to bed.

I go to bed. You're in some trouble here, sister. You're in some pretty bad trouble..

"Hey, it's Sunday, we should do something? Do you want to go for a drive? Let's head east, over towards Worcester, we can drive by that pretty lake? I know you like to be by the water, we will stop at that café we drove by last month. What a pretty drive that will be. Now, stop all that writing and come on, I get a chance to have you, too, you know. The next book isn't due until March, that draft isn't due until October, you can give me one afternoon by the water, can't you?"

I throw my head back and laugh gaily. "OH YOU," I say. "Alright, just this one, then tomorrow I really have to get back at it. But yes, today is yours."

I dress in a white roadster outfit (I don't even know what a white roadster outfit is, but for the purposes of this sequence, I want it to be that). I toss a gauzy white scarf around my scarlet locks and off we go.

"How beautiful you are today," he says. I look at him and lower my eyes modestly. He is also dressed in a roadster outfit (God knows, I don't know). He has always been kind and lovely to me. We talk, we laugh, the wind is through our hair.

The café is on the lake. It is a little before noon, so it hasn't filled up yet. I can tell the hostess recognizes me, a secret smile as she leads us to a table by the window. He pulls my chair out.

I haul out of the pickup, stumble to the nearest table and fall into a chair. I toss my purse to the empty side of the table, yammer something about a Bloody Mary to the perky blonde waitperson.

I look over the lake. It is somewhat overcast. There is a deck outside and one lower, to the right. The servers are huddled in a gaggle around the end of the bar, gearing up for the shift. They are not talking about me.

"Oh yes, it is good to get away for a time, aren't you clever by half? You are so right, I did need a break from publishers, deadlines and all that."

(I also think of taking a break from line-learning, directors, opening night jitters and realize I am mixing up artistic areas, but I don't care. I have to give him a name today, I'll call him Jay, Jay doesn't care. Though it is a sign that this particular dream ballet is wearing thin. No matter, take it as far as it will go.)

"When are you going into the City?" he asks.

"Well, I guess I should scoot in next week, what do you think? I do need to get in to see Sid (the agent) and he and the team need to look at these last two chapters before they send it to the publisher."

Jesus Christ it's hot in here. Where is that Bloody Mary? Well, at least I'm by the water. I haven't seen a soul in two days. God this weekend is endless. One more day of this? I'd rather be working.

"Hahaha, darling, look at that charming little paddleboat, over there. How do those ladies hold on, dressed in those long white day dresses and clutching those parasols?" I laugh gaily (again) and toss back my scarlet locks (again).

I should have washed my hair. When was the last time I washed my hair? I rummage for a scrunchie. This purse is too big, loose change, gas receipts, broken makeup compacts that it is far too late for. I find a scrunchie balled up and attempt to wad some hair through it.

The Bloody Mary arrives. The blond waitperson cheerily asks me if I'm ready. Am I ready?

I blubber up something like fish and chips and off she goes.

I look back at the lake. I see a duck family, mama and paddling babies. There is a speedboat hauling a jet-skier. That looks like fun. I wish I could swim.

The lake reminds me of the camp. Dad would like it here. Though he would say it is fancy, for the sports. Will I ever bring him out of the home, to a place on a lake again, for lunch? Probably not. It's too much work, I'm selfish, I'm not doing enough, I'm not trying hard enough. Before the first Bloody Mary sip, I start to cry.

"Why don't I come into the City with you," he says? "After you meet with Sid, we can see a show, or that new ballet?"
"Oh darling," I say, "no need really, I am just in and out. I'll be back Thursday."
He looks crestfallen, there in his roadster whites. "Really, I will be so busy with these meetings, and I do hate dragging you along for them, you'll be so bored."
He looks down, pushing his radicchio around the plate.

Blah Blah, you're not trying hard enough, you're selfish, yeah yeah, you're in a public place, pull yourself together. I stop crying for a minute. I discreetly (I think) wipe my face. I look back at the lake. More people are out in boats. Kids are running on the banks. The café is filling up. The fish and chips arrive and I am presentable enough to look away from the window, nod directly to whom, whom? Amy is her name.

"Thank you, Amy, no nothing else, thank you." Her bright smile dims a bit and she glances back at me as she slips away.

Fuck. Now it's a thing, now I'm sitting here crying and it's a thing for the staff. Fuck. I turn back to the window, to the Georges Seurat world beyond the glass. I push away all the I'm-a-Terrible-Daughter-Can't-Even-Take-Your-Father-Out-To-a-Nice-Lunch-by-a-Lake-That-You-Know-He-Would-Like terrors.

A forkful of friséehalfway lifted, he says, "I don't understand why you won't let me in that part of your life. Why can't I see your New York friends, go along to the agent's office? I could be helpful, you know, in negotiations." His blond hair, his gleaming teeth, his puppy dog eyes, truth be told, were getting tiresome. He's not usually the type I go for, what was I thinking?

"Darling, I am perfectly capable of negotiating, you know that, silly. I think I'm going to the opera, you don't like the opera." I see him getting upset, the corners of his mouth start to tremble. "Oh darling, really, don't be that way. I'll be back in a few days, I need a little space to handle my business affairs and to see friends. In fact, I need a little more space in general. Can't you see that..."

Wait a minute, wait a minute, am I fighting with my imaginary boyfriend? I am breaking up, in a bit of a scene...with my imaginary boyfriend?

I pull my tear-stained face off the glass separating me from the Sunday in the Park world. I pull back errant strands of dirty hair fallen from the scrunchie. I look down at the fish and chips. I cry harder. The gaggle of staff near the bar collectively look at me, collectively slightly turn away. Amy breaks off and glides over. She slips me napkins and I mop down my face. I calm myself enough to look around, thinking I am presentable. A biker slips into a nearby table. He doesn't notice me. I am calm enough to eat a couple of bites. No, I'm not calm enough after all. I turn back to the window, the lake.

There is a family outside, in Seurat world, at one of the picnic tables. Kids, a dog, a goofy, shaggy dog. They are taking pictures and they corral the dog in the center of the shot. I wonder if it's the dog's birthday.

I wipe my face again. I can get down half the fish. You're not presentable and you need to leave. You are a mess and you shouldn't be in public. You need to get a grip, you really do. Leave the food, leave the drink. I signal for the check. It quickly appears. I hand over a card, no, you can just take it, I don't need to see the total. I get up to leave, the gaggle looks away. I think I hear them sigh in relief. The biker has a draft beer and is looking out the window. At the door, I look back. I see him in a fleeting instant: his head in his hands, sunglasses off, white roadster jacket over his chair. I turn away.

I hoist myself up into the pickup (not the smart MG). Still crying, but not as badly, I back out. No scarf on my scarlet locks, my scrunchie falls out. At a light, I tie back my hair. I look over to the empty passenger seat. I drive the pickup back to the house, alone.

Monday, Memorial Day. I stop at the supermarket to pick up some things. VA Ray was outside, handing out the red poppies. He hands me a couple. "No. No need to make a donation," he says. "Thank your father for his service."

I drive the backroads to the Shady Rest.

"Hi Dad. Hey, I ran into Ray at Stop and Shop. You remember Ray, from the VA? He came to the house a few months ago and helped us with the VA benefits?"

I know he doesn't remember, but he says he does.

"Well, Ray asked me to give you a poppy, it's Memorial Day. Ray says thank you for your service."

"Oh, that's nice."

We sit for a few more minutes, not talking.

"OK, Dad, get some sleep." I turn on the TV for him and leave.

When I get back to the house, I start calling doctors.

AN ABANDONED FARM IN NORTHERN NEW HAMPSHIRE

John Grey

The farm is long abandoned.

What were once fields

is now wilderness.

The grass is so high

it's buried a rusty tractor

and is now working on

the dilapidated barn.

And the trees are moving in.

In years to come,

they'll swallow up

the homestead with the sunken roof.

According to the swallows in the eaves,

this old house is a tree already.

Elsewhere, civilization

rips up, shreds, the natural world,

remakes the landscape

in its own image.

I've seen the earthmovers,

the scaffolding, the cranes.

I've heard the jackhammers,

the cussing of men and women

in hard hats.

Destruction, building,

is always in a hurry.

But here the process takes its time.

Where corn grew poorly,

trout lily thrives.

Where a farmer struggled

to put food on the table,

a deer leads her fawn

to the succulent growth

at forest's edge.

Where a family once gave up

on their acreage,

a bygone history repeats itself.

DECADES AGO

Jamie McDonough

Decades ago,

when special needs school I started attending.

I immediately came to know

my days of summer vacation were ending.

I wish I had been more happy in those days.

but I wasn't taking to my new lifestyle.

We would go on fieldtrips to many a nice place.

I wish back then, I felt more often like a smile.

I was upset that every day of summer I had to go to program.

We would gather in a big van and go somewhere fun.

I wish I was as willing as I am now,

instead of just wishing for each day to be done.

But I think I always tried to be nice.

I had my share of fun,

and wish I had taken my parents' advice,

making the most of my days, every one.

Looking back, I don't remember complaining

to anyone outside the program and immediate family.

I have to admit my days were not that full of pain.

I know this poem's kind of a downer,

but you'll have to believe me.

After all, I was just sulking, mostly.

People who had it worse, I feel bad for them.

At the end of the day I can almost speak boastfully,

because I never really had a problem.

THERE ONCE WAS AN ENORMOUS SNAKE

Jamie McDonough

There once was an enormous snake

that when it ate cake,

it's utensils were a shovel and a rake.

However, something was wrong with this poem.

Maybe to you it had already been known.

Snakes have no arms and hands to call their own.

How can I pass off a poem with such a glaring mistake?

A snake would just swallow a cake.

But I wanted to rhyme something with cake,

shovel and rake.

What if I use a drake?

But a drake's wings can't hold a shovel and a rake,

so that idea's half baked.

I'm sorry I couldn't give you a proper poem for now.

Will you have this one anyhow?

And the next one will be more worthy

of the brain behind my eyebrows.

PATHWAYS OF IMAGINATION

Science Fiction, Fantasy, and Paranormal Writing

ETERNAL VERMONT

Shonna Ryan

A Ford Model T passed by at too fast a speed, and it pushed a wave of icy water over the top of John's boots. He tried to lift his feet out of the way, but there was nothing to be done. The cold water splashed up over his ankles and dampened the cuffs of his trousers before seeping through the leather of his boots and into the wool socks beneath.

He cast a frown in the direction of the retreating vehicle, but he didn't bother to shout or swear after the driver. That wasn't really his way. John stood just over six feet tall and already needed to shave daily at the age of eighteen, and although he had been called a brute when it came to sports, he was a quiet man in daily life. He just continued to stand there in the sleet, his feet quickly growing cold.

The sign in John's hands read "Abigail." He wasn't sure if the girl he was waiting for went by a shortened version of the name, nor what her last name was; he had only just learned of her existence a month prior. His guardian, an enigmatic man named Wilbur Sparrow, had shown up out of the blue at the end of John's first semester at Boston University. John had received word amidst a blizzard that Mr. Sparrow was in the city and wished to meet his ward for dinner. It had been an even colder day than this one when John tramped through the snow to meet Mr. Sparrow at an upscale Parisian-style restaurant. It wasn't the type of food John preferred, but he owed his education and many opportunities besides to Mr. Sparrow, so he said nothing as they sat down to eat.

Mr. Sparrow was a man with a stern disposition, a nearly bald head, and a long nose. He had taken John in as his ward when he was eight years old, yet they had only seen each other less than a dozen times over the past ten years. Why Mr. Sparrow had chosen John as his ward was a complete mystery; the man had never explained anything he did, and John thought it improper to ask. Dinner was a quiet affair, with stiff questions about John's studies, the weather and such. As Mr. Sparrow stood to take his leave, he simply said, "You will need to take next semester off. I've arranged for the family to spend some time in Vermont at an estate I recently purchased."

This simple statement had floored John. Not only was John expected to drop his studies and end his hockey season, but because in their ten years of acquaintance, Mr. Sparrow had never mentioned the word "family." John knew that Mr. Sparrow had a rather pretty wife; he had seen outdated pictures of her hanging about the townhouse in Boston. While John was polite to a fault, his curiosity had compelled him to ask the housekeeper about Mr. Sparrow once or twice. Still, she'd provided little to no information aside from to say that Mr. Sparrow was a very successful international businessman and that he primarily lived just outside Washington D.C. with Mrs. Sparrow. She went on to declare, "Aren't you just the luckiest boy who ever lived to be sponsored by such a great man?"

John considered himself bright enough, but he had always been slow with words. Before he could respond to Mr. Sparrow's sudden statement, the thin-faced man quickly mentioned that the rest of the details would be arriving by mail in the coming weeks, "And oh, don't forget about Abigail."

Of course, John had no idea who Abigail was.

A week later, a package arrived with directions to the estate in Vermont. The letter included simply explained that Abigail was Mr. Sparrow's ward who lived in England. John was to meet her ocean liner, the RMS Samaria, at the pier on the given time and date, and two train tickets were provided for the trip. And so, John stood on the dock in soaking wet boots, waiting for a girl whom he knew nothing of.

When the Samaria docked, John waited with his sign, his cap pulled down low to keep the sleet from his eyes as he scanned the disembarking crowd for a girl traveling alone. He imagined she would be young, perhaps the age he was when Mr. Sparrow had taken him in. It was for this reason that he was quite shocked when a beautiful young woman cleared her throat to draw his attention and pointed to his sign.

"Are you John?" she asked, amusement dancing in her light brown eyes. Her accent was melodic, and he was embarrassed when the cold weather caused his own voice to come out raspy upon voicing the affirmative. "I'm Abigail; everyone calls me Abi though. But I suppose Wil didn't bother to tell you that. If I had to guess, Wil didn't bother to tell you much of anything."

It took John a moment to sort out that Wil was in reference to Mr. Wilbur Sparrow, and though he'd only known Abi for mere seconds, he already felt like a dull lunk of a man in her presence. "Do you have any luggage?" he asked when he found his tongue.

"Yes, of course," she smiled, and pointed to where the luggage was being unloaded so that John could have the driver bring the car around. It turned out she had two very heavy trunks that John had to help the driver strap to the back of the car. It wasn't until they were settled warmly into the train's passenger car that he learned she was studying at Oxford University, and she simply couldn't bear to be so far away from all her books.

Once on the train, she launched into a flurry of information about how Wil had taken her under his care when she was six. She mainly had spent her time in boarding schools, and she had never been to the United States before. For the most part, John had just nodded along mutely. His wet socks made his feet itch, and it wasn't until they switched trains in Springfield that he had the chance to change into something dry.

Feeling a bit more confident, he endeavored to say, "So, how do you like Oxford?"

She gushed for a while about all of her studies (she seemed to be studying just about everything) and then concluded by saying, "And don't say anything about it being peculiar for women to study at University. Oxford has admitted women at full membership since 1920."

"I wasn't going to say anything of the sort," he insisted. "Boston University has had female students for over fifty years ... since the 1870s, I believe." She looked surprised by this, and John was elated to know something that she did not. He had a feeling that moments like these would be a rarity as he got to know her.

Not wanting to ruin his intelligent moment, John proceeded to look out the window as they rolled into the scenic Green Mountains. The sun was setting as the train chugged through the valleys, and it was the perfect New England winter sunset; brilliant shades of yellow and orange melting into snowy peaks as dark pine trees flitted past the windowpane. He glanced over to see that Abi had gone silent as well, her eyes wide as she took in the scenery. She caught him looking at her. She smiled and seemed to blush, but that might have been a trick of the light.

The sun had set behind the mountains when they arrived at their stop, and the stars were starting to appear in the deep purple sky overhead. The town they disembarked at had nothing on the hustle and bustle of Boston, but it wasn't sleepy either. Trucks piled with thick logs rumbled into town, rowdy granite miners poured into a local restaurant, and the smell of smoke from wood stoves filled the air. A car and a driver waited for them, and John once more assisted with securing their belongings before they took off to Mr. Sparrow's estate.

It was quite dark as they left the town's center, and the roads were so bumpy that at one point, they hit a hole so hard they were nearly launched from their seats. Abi reached for John's hand but quickly withdrew it when she realized they were not going to die, and she diverted her embarrassment by asking the driver where precisely they were headed.

"Oh, the Ballard Mansion is a good way out of town," the man said, his accent a peculiar dialect that reminded John of some Canadians he played hockey with.

"Mansion?" Abi asked, excitement clear in her tone.

"Ay, yup," the driver responded. "The Ballard family built the mansion back at the turn of the century. They made their fortune off the granite once the trains finally made their way up here."

"Where are they now?" Abi asked.

There was a long pause, and then the driver said, "We're almost there." The cheery tone with which he had spoken before had vanished, and even in the dark, John could see Abi give him a confused look.

They crossed a wood-covered bridge and emerged from the forest and into a clearing on which a massive home stood. The pale moonlight cast shadows across the steep rooftops and white smoke against black sky emanated from several chimney stacks. Gas lamps flickered from the pillars of the front entrance. The car pulled up to a set of double doors constructed of wood so dark that they appeared to be nearly black. This time, John did not need to help with the luggage because two young men seemed to spring out of the night air and hurriedly assisted in delivering the trunks into the house.

***

John and Abi entered into a main foyer that was entirely lined by wood paneling as dark as the front doors. Although a gas-lit chandelier provided light, it somehow did not seem to reach the shadowy corners of the room. John found himself gravitating towards the fire, which blazed in a nearby hearth. It's just the cold mountain air, he told himself as a chill ran up his spine.

"You're right on time!" exclaimed a cheery voice with an accent similar to that of their driver. John glanced up the grand staircase at the shadowy end of the foyer, and a plump woman with grey hair pulled back in a tight bun descended towards them. She had a hearty look to her, like one who had learned to survive many a harsh winter, but there was merriment in her dark eyes. "I'm Mrs. Emerson. Allow me to show you to your respective rooms, and then the dinner table will be set. The rest of the family is already here."

Again John wondered, what family? But he said nothing as he followed her up the stairs and down a hallway lined with large portrait paintings of sour-looking individuals. Once Abi had been shown to her room, they arrived at his own a few doors down; a large bedroom with a four-post bed, a maple wood desk, and a fire already roaring in the hearth. John quickly unpacked his belongings into an overly large armoire and then proceeded to clean up and dress for dinner.

On the way to the dining room, he got lost several times, despite Mrs. Emerson's explicit directions. The house was a maze of barely lit corridors and seemingly endless staircases. As he turned a corner, he found himself in yet another passageway so dark that he needed to run his hand along the wall to keep from bumping into anything. Feeling a strip of molding beneath his hand, he walked cautiously at first, picking up pace as he felt certain he heard breathing coming from the darkness. The hairs on the back of his neck stood on end as he half jogged towards the dim light at the end of the corridor. Then his fingertips brushed against something warm and alive.

His heart was hammering against his chest with fright but when he heard a familiar scream he stopped himself from flailing out blindly into the darkness. "Abi?" he asked of the silhouette standing just feet in front of him.

"I'm here," she said, but her voice was not coming from the shadowy figure in front of him; she was standing behind him. John reached his hand out ever so slowly towards the unmoving silhouette before him, his fingers turning icy cold the closer they reached out into the darkness. He felt Abi grasp his elbow, and he dropped his hand, turning to face her in the darkness. When he looked back again, the figure was gone.

"Maybe I'm being silly, but this place is a bit ... disconcerting," Abi said, now slipping her arm through his so they could proceed down the hallway side-by-side.

"It gives me the creeps," he admitted, and she laughed. At the end of the hallway, they were greeted by light. John looked at her to see why she was laughing. "Are you making fun of me?"

"No, not at all!" she responded, looking aghast. "It's just the way you said it ... your accent, I mean." He shuffled his feet uncomfortably. As a child, he'd had a rather notable Boston accent, and he'd tried to tame it over the years, but it still slipped out. He imagined it sounded thuggish next to her refined British accent, but she added, "I like your accent. It's rather cute."

They entered the dining room, and already four people were seated at the overly large table. At the head sat Mr. Sparrow, and at his right hand was a woman who John immediately recognized from the pictures as Mrs. Sparrow. She now had many grey streaks through her raven hair, but she was still quite beautiful. Across from her sat two children, a boy and a girl, perhaps four or five years old. They were dressed very nicely for dinner; the little boy had the serious demeanor of an old soul, but the little girl tugged at her braid and looked eager to be done with dinner and go play.

John took a seat next to Mrs. Sparrow, who smiled at him, but her smile was not reflected in her eyes. He became caught up in her sad gaze for a moment when Mr. Sparrow said, "Greetings" in a tone as dry and unaffected as ever. He introduced everyone; the little boy and girl were called James and Helena.

Dinner commenced; a delicious feast of turkey and roasted vegetables. There was a pudding for dessert, and nobody spoke much except to note that travel had gone smoothly and there was a storm about to come in.

"You're unusually quiet, Abi," Mr. Sparrow said after the dishes were cleared away.

Abi attempted to stifle a yawn. "I suppose it's been a long day. I woke up at sea just this morning, and now here I am in the mountains! The marvels of modern travel."

"Quite," Mr. Sparrow said with an inclination of his head. "Mrs. Sparrow, I'd imagine you'll want to take the little ones off to bed as well." Mrs. Sparrow said nothing, simply nodding, and the children rose with her, little Helena running to the door and James giving the room a final, concerned look before following. John stood to rise as well, but Mr. Sparrow said, "I'd like a word with you before you retire, son."

John gave a start at the use of the word *son* but nodded in consent, and Abi gave him an unreadable look before following the rest of the so-called family out of the room. "Are those your children?" John asked after the silence welling up beneath the crackling of the fire became too much to stand.

"You are all my children in a manner of speaking," Mr. Sparrow said, fixing his dark eyes on John. "But no, they are not our biological children. You see John, many years ago there was a terrible tragedy in our home in D.C. A fire. And my wife … well, she was growing old to start a new family and was too heartbroken. I, however, missed the sound of children's laughter, and so I took you and Abi under my wing."

This statement dumbfounded John. The sound of children's laughter? Even when he had been young enough to be considered a child, Mr. Sparrow had never been in his presence long enough to witness him laugh or play. He'd never even seen one of his sports matches.

Mr. Sparrow continued. "But then, just a few months ago, Mrs. Sparrow had a sudden change of heart. She lamented her quiet life in Virginia and said she wanted to be a family once more. So we adopted little James and Helena. I purchased this property, and now we can spend some time, all together, as a proper family. Abi is about a year older than you, but I hold it to you to keep an eye over all of your siblings as the eldest brother. Keep them safe." These last words came out dark and nearly menacing, and this time John was certain that the chill up his spine had nothing to do with the cold mountain air.

"Yes, sir," was all John could manage, his head whirring. These people were not his family; he had no family. He had been born an orphan, and this was all madness. Yet, he did owe Mr. Sparrow a great debt. So he supposed playing family for a few months in beautiful Vermont wasn't the worst thing the man could ask for in repayment.

The next few weeks passed with a deep tension. Elaborate meals were had in the dining room, but the rest of the day involved everyone retreating into their separate corners of the mansion. The short winter days did nothing to ease the unsettling energy about the household; while the sunlight was out, John found he could enjoy a few pleasant hours snowshoeing the surrounding property or reading a book by the fire. But then the darkness would return, and the shadows seemed to swallow up any joy that could be found in the household. The nights were the worst of it all.

The first night, John had been unable to sleep. A storm kicked up and had the wind howling at the shutters of his bedroom. At times there seemed to be a nearly human moan mixed in with the noise. The children had both wailed that night, but when he went to them, Mrs. Sparrow was already there, soothing them back to sleep with that same sad, empty look in her eyes. When he returned to his bedroom, he had nearly fallen asleep when the scratching sound began.

At first, it was faint and could hardly be heard over the wailing of the wind. Then it escalated, and he realized that it was coming from inside the armoire where he had stored his clothing. Sitting up in bed, he stared into the darkness, the dying embers of the fire providing just enough light to make out the shape of the bulky piece of furniture, and yet he was sure that not only was there scratching, but the doors were rattling as though something was trapped inside. Steeling his nerve, he jumped from the bed and flung the doors open, prepared to find a mouse or perhaps a rat, but when he opened the armoire, nothing was inside, but his neatly hung clothing. When he closed the doors once more, the sound stopped, and he finally rested, but it would happen again nearly every night.

It was a cold but brilliantly sunny day when he discovered the ice skates hanging in the mansion's recreational shed; four pairs; two in adult sizes and the other two made for children. Spurred by a wonderful idea, he shoveled clear the swimming hole in the backyard, which was frozen solid. His efforts yielded a perfect field of ice, and he ran back to the house, first rousing Abi.

Abi had grown increasingly quiet since arriving at Ballard Mansion, only leaving her room to attend family meals. She had become somewhat pale and quite unlike the excitable woman he had met in Boston. After rapping on her bedroom door, Abi dully gave him permission to enter. He found her in an armchair by the fire, her feet tucked up beneath her as she read. She pulled a woolen shawl close around her shoulders and gave him a quizzical look as he explained about the ice skating opportunity he had put together.

"I've never skated before," she responded, but there was a light in her eyes once more as he promised to teach her. It was quite easy to convince Helena to don her winter wear, and although James seemed less convinced of the idea, he came around to it.

Once outside, John was thrilled to be back on the ice. He skated a few quick circuits to warm up as Helena and Abi cheered him on. He helped James and Helena get their skates fastened and led them out to the ice. Even James showed a rare smile at the experience. Once they were off on their own, sliding about in a mostly safe fashion, he turned his attention to Abi, who was stagger stepping out onto the ice with a fierce look of determination on her face. He guessed she was the sort who had never failed at anything before and refused to do so now. Abi took a few tentative glides and seemed to be getting the hang of it when she hit a rut in the ice and pitched forward. Fortunately, John was nearby and caught her easily, and while he'd expected her to tense up at his assistance, she instead wrapped her arms around his shoulders and tossed her head back, laughing at the clear blue sky above.

The skating experience brought about a change to the feel of the mansion, at least during the daytime hours. Abi and John took to assisting Mrs. Sparrow with teaching the young children, and dinners became far more lively, with even Mrs. Sparrow laughing on occasion as the children shared stories about what they had learned. Mr. Sparrow's affection did not change, but he would nod his head and listen intently before retreating to his study, as was his habit whenever meals were not being shared.

The nights, however, were still filled with frightening things. Once, in hushed tones, Helena told John about a little boy who would sit at the foot of their bed every night, crying. John would have excused it for a child's imagination gone wild, but the somber James corroborated the story. John made passing mention of this to Abi, and she set into a flurry of activity, determined to learn more about the house's history and the family who had lived there before. She tried to ask all of the groundskeepers about the Ballard family, and of course, she did her best to quiz Mrs. Emerson, but everyone remained as tight-lipped as the driver had been upon their arrival.

When spring came, and the snow melted, John realized he had become quite stir crazy. While he wouldn't be due back to school until the Fall, he needed to get out of the house. Abi felt quite the same and weaponizing her best sweet-talking tactics she convinced Mr. Sparrow to allow them to take Helena and James into town for an afternoon to see a Charlie Chaplin film at the theatre. However, when they got to town, she left John to mind the children and took off on her own, determined to learn something about the Ballard family.

When the movie ended, they met up at a nearby diner for a treat. Abi looked pale-faced and troubled. "What's wrong?" John asked her while the children were occupied picking out which type of pie they wanted.

"I'll tell you later," she mumbled and then proceeded to push a piece of cake around her plate for the next half hour while the kids regaled her with Charlie's on-screen antics.

When they returned to Ballard Mansion, John wanted to get her alone right away to ask what she had learned, but Mr. Sparrow had dictated that there would be afternoon tea and nobody was to skip out. During tea, Mr. Sparrow seemed to be exceptionally vigilant as his dark eyes darted from Abi and John to the children and then back again.

Even after tea time had passed, John was unable to get Abi alone, and he didn't see her again until dinner. She still looked distraught as they ate their meal, but if Mr. Sparrow noticed, he made no comment. He did, however, insist that John join him for an after-dinner smoke, even inviting him into his office, which nobody had been allowed to enter up until that point. Abi gave John a nearly panicked look as he acquiesced to the invitation, but he wasn't sure what else she'd have him do.

The inside of Mr. Sparrow's office was elaborate, bookshelves lining the walls from floor to ceiling, and each stuffed with so many books that John was certain Abi's eyes would pop out if she saw. At the front of the room, a massive, marble encased fireplace held roaring flames, and before it sat two wing-backed armchairs. They each took a seat, and John noticed that above the mantle hung a portrait of Mrs. Sparrow, depicted in dark, heavy brush strokes.

"Mr. Sparrow," John said slowly. "If you don't mind me asking, do you have any pictures of your children? I mean the ones you lost. I should very much like to see them."

"I don't keep such pictures around anymore," Mr. Sparrow said in a dour tone. "It upsets Mrs. Sparrow's frail disposition."

"Oh, of course," John replied, but it still struck him as fairly peculiar. Despite whatever tragedy befell them, it seemed unnatural to want to hide away the memory of their own children.

"Are you happy here, John?" Mr. Sparrow asked suddenly, handing John a cigar.

"Of course," John answered quickly, not wanting to seem ungrateful. "I mean, I look forward to returning to my studies this Fall, but this has been an enjoyable respite from the city."

Mr. Sparrow flicked a match against a striker with such force that for a moment John thought the man might mean to burn him with it. Slowly, he pulled the flame back and lit John's cigar. "I would like to ask you to stay here until the end of the year. James and Helena have grown quite attached to you, so Mrs. Sparrow tells me. And I think if you stay a little longer, you could really learn to love a place like this. So serene. So silent."

Mr. Sparrow seemed to fall into a trance, puffing his cigar as he watched the flames dance in the hearth. John was thankful for the quiet opportunity to try to string some words together. This whole trip was already preposterous, but the idea he should spend the entirety of a year so far from his home, his education, and his hockey was utter lunacy. He was about to tell Mr. Sparrow as much, good manners be damned, but then he thought of Abi. Would she be staying here until the year's end? While he wanted to go back to his old life, the thought of leaving her behind pained him somehow.

"I'd like a bit to think upon it if you don't mind," John said, and Mr. Sparrow just gave a curt nod, his black eyes unblinking as he gazed deeper and deeper into the flames. When John extinguished his cigar and made his excuses, Mr. Sparrow did not even seem to notice.

John practically ran back to his room, his heart racing. Something was very wrong. While part of him had known that from the moment he stepped foot inside the Ballard Mansion, it was only really setting in now. He paced his room until he was certain he must have worn a pattern in the rug. Then a knocking came on his door. He jumped at the noise and reached for a fire poker as a weapon before he could even register what he was doing. The door flew open.

Abi raced inside, closing the door shut in her wake and wrapping her arms around him. She was shaking ever so slightly, and he held her, not certain what to say. As usual, she spoke first to fill the silence. "John, the family who lived here before, the Ballard's ... they murdered their children and then killed themselves.

A cold chill seeped through his bones. "I knew something felt just ... wrong about this place," he responded, and despite the vagary in his response, she seemed to understand what he was saying. He told her about the scratching sounds coming from his closet, and she told him about a woman's voice that whispered from the chimney just before dawn, singing a sweet lullaby and weeping before fading away. Abi shuddered when she finished recounting the tale, and he pulled a quilt from his bed to wrap around her shoulders.

"There is no doubt that this place has a bad energy. Mr. Sparrow wants me to stay here until year's end," he told her, feeling indignant once more.

"He asked the same of me" she frowned, standing beside John as he stoked the fire. "I wanted to leave to return in time for summer studies at Oxford, but he told me it wouldn't be possible to arrange my passage home until year's end. Oh, and he added, wouldn't I like to stay awhile longer anyhow?" She let out a short, humorless laugh. "So he's basically got me trapped here until further notice. I have no means of returning to England on my own."

John felt heated at this; Sparrow had no right to keep Abi his de facto prisoner. At least John could leave whenever he wanted; he had enough money to take the train back to Boston should he need to make his own way. But he would not leave Abi there alone. He told her as much, and to his great surprise, she turned to him and kissed him.

"Can I stay here tonight, John?" she asked, her eyes hopeful. "I'm frightened."

He kissed her as a way of response.

And so summer came to pass, and while the darkness inside the walls of Ballard Mansion did not disappear, it did abate somewhat. The days were longer, and despite the unprecedented amount of rain that came that summer, there were still many sunny Vermont days to be had hiking through the forests, learning to drive about the grounds, going fishing with James, and cooling off in the swimming hole at the end of it all. Then, at night, he had Abi, and that was so wonderful that the unnatural chill that ran through the house did not affect him as cruelly as it once had.

As the leaves changed color and a splendid Vermont fall settled upon them, John and Abi resumed discussions about leaving Ballard Mansion. He wondered at his options of studying abroad in England,

and she thought perhaps she could see what courses Boston University had to offer. As the days grew shorter and colder, their desire to leave became almost frantic, and John found himself counting down to the end of the year.

November came upon them, and the rain poured down worse than ever. Dinner that night was a somber affair. The relentless pattern of rain against the windows seemed to have everyone's nerves on edge. When Mrs. Sparrow suddenly asked Abi to join her in the parlor after dinner, John thought nothing of it. He suspected Mrs. Sparrow and Abi would discuss arrangements for Abi's safe return to Oxford. But when he passed the parlor on the way to his room, he heard raised voices, and he paused to listen.

"It's not right; it's not natural," Mrs. Sparrow was saying. "He's your brother."

"He's NOT my brother!" Abi replied, a tone of incredulous laughter in her voice. "We are not related by blood or even by law! None of us here are actual family, however much you might like to pretend it. John and I are leaving at the end of the year. If Wil refuses to honor our agreement, we'll make our own way."

There was a loud slap, and now John was racing towards the parlor. He threw the doors open in time to see Abi tussling with Mrs. Sparrow. He moved quickly to intervene, but was not quick enough. Abi pushed Mrs. Sparrow off of her, and the older woman staggered back. Her head slammed against the side of the hearth and blood spurted from the wound instantly. Her blood hit the embers of the fire with a sickening sizzling noise.

Abi let out a strangled gasp, realizing immediately that Mrs.

Sparrow was dead. John drew Abi to him, and just then, Mr. Sparrow entered the room. Seeing his wife's prone body by the hearth, a look of shock crossed his face. It was the most expression John had ever seen from the man. But just as quickly as it was there, it disappeared.

"Well, this changes things," he said in almost a bored tone, and John unconsciously placed himself between Mr. Sparrow and the now-weeping Abi. "I was going to wait a bit longer, but tonight is as good as any night."

"It was an accident," John said, and he was relieved to hear confidence in his tone.

Mr. Sparrow paid him no mind, and he passed by his wife's unmoving corpse to grab a fire prod from beside the mantle. Inspecting it, he said, "My good friend Joseph Ballard built this mansion. A month or so before he killed his family, and himself, he told me that the house was special; that it can trap spirits within its walls forever. How wonderful, he thought, would it be to ensure that one could keep their family together forever. Then Joseph shot the children while they slept, and his wife jumped from the rooftop. Joseph chose to hang himself in his bedroom's armoire. Naturally, I thought he was mad. And yet, having lost my own children so tragically, I could not stop thinking about it. How wonderful indeed to be able to keep your family together forever. It's too late for my first family. But this new family I have built ... we can all share eternity."

Mr. Sparrow turned quickly, swinging the poker in a wide arch that John narrowly dodged. Hurling himself at the older man, the two of them fell to the floor, wrestling in Mrs. Sparrow's still-warm blood. "Run!" John urged Abi, and he barely managed to choke the words out; Mr. Sparrow was far stronger than he looked.

Their fight seemed to go on for an impossible amount of time. The poker was pressed between the two of them and Mr. Sparrow's spittle flew into John's face as he put his every ounce of energy into pushing John off of him. John pushed down, harder and harder, until slowly the metal poker was resting against Mr. Sparrow's neck. Still, John pushed harder, and the man's long face began to turn purple. His black eyes bulged, and he began to twitch. Even still, John pushed down harder, and there was a crunching sound from within Mr. Sparrow's throat, and the twitching stopped.

Abi was screaming his name, and John looked up, in a daze, the world spinning around him. Abi was in the foyer, helping the kids hurry into boots and coats. When she saw him, she choked back a sob of relief. "We need to get out of here, John," she said, her voice frantic. He grabbed the car keys from their peg, threw his feet into galoshes that didn't even belong to him, and led them out into the pouring rain.

The rain was coming down in sheets, battering against the muddy, soaked ground in a vicious assault. John's boot sunk into the mud and stuck so badly that he could not pull his foot free. For a panicked moment, he felt certain the Earth was about to suck him down into its mucky soil, to devour him alive. But he pulled his foot free of the boot. With only one boot on, he splashed over and got the car started, helping get the children seated as expediently as he could.

He worried that the car might get stuck in the mud, but it powered through. Although the night was pitch black, and although rain obscured the windshield, they moved quickly across the property and towards the covered bridge.

One thousand two hundred and eighty-five bridges would later be reported as having been swept away by the Great Vermont Flood of 1927. In the darkness John had no way to see that the covered bridge had been washed away. As they tipped over the edge and plummeted into the black river beneath, his last thought was that at least his eternity would include Abigail.

TO HILLY FIELDS

Kate Meyer-Currey

We often went for walks here,

Near my grandparents' home

Off the Lexden Road, common ground

Spread out like a toga over the Roman road

Which marched to the town's suburban

Margins, with its acreage of scuffed grass

And meandering paths fortified with concrete

Gun emplacements left over from the war

Stood implacable, silent; watchful.

Something of unease was present:

Not openly voiced in the muffled 'Seventies',

Where children were somehow freer to roam

In places adults shun now, unless they are

Together. I went off alone

At ten or eleven years old—I don't remember.

My Clarks sandals knew the pavements well

I was often at the town museum, peering

Into the murky depths of a covered well or

Staring down mummy-cases, to show I had

No fear of the long-dead bandaged inhabitants.

I knew they were harmless to me,

Even though they haunted my child's imagination;

Like the spot at the head of the attic stair

Where shadows flickered on the long mirror,

Reflecting only Stygian darkness.

Once my grandfather gave me

A veiled warning not to go

To Hilly Fields by myself

As 'something bad had happened there.'

So I went, uncertain, hesitant, and curious.

But I saw no one that day,

And while I walked upon that bumpy terrain,

I was prepared for anything to happen.

I will never understand why I made myself prey,

In my short summer dress and knee-socks.

I could hear the loudness of my breath;

My pumping heart, felt the blank gaze

Of sniper slits, when I decided to turn back.

I never did go back there alone.

I am certain a rank of silent centurions shielded me

Guarding my naive unheeding.

At fifty-one, I look back at my younger self,

Disbelieving I could take such risks

Given the world we live in now.

So uneasy am I now when I recall

That childhood exploration,

My passive defiance of adults' muted fear, that

Looking backwards, over my shoulder,

Discomfort still persists.

I had a lucky escape from the thing unspoken,

That lay like a shadow over Hilly Fields,

Following in my every footstep.

PEOPLE RUNNING NAKED THROUGH THE SNOWY WOODS

William Doreski

Why are all these people running

naked through the snowy woods?

Driving from Petersham to Hardwick

in the shallow January light

I encounter this phenomenon.

Sleek men and women, obese

men and women, adolescents,

children running pink and brown,

panting through the knee-deep snow

toward the frozen Quabbin Reservoir.

I park in a turnout and watch

the naked flesh pout and pucker

with clumsy stride, momentum

flopping them face-down only

to rise gasping and slogging forward.

The people of several townships

must have caught this fervor. I follow

along a plowed road they avoid

although it parallels their route

to the reservoir. The rigid

shadows of the leafless forest
cage the scene. Small brooks furrow
the otherwise perfect snow
these desperate nudes are trampling.

When I recall the most sinister
photographs of the last World War
I almost drop to my knees
with horror. The large flat expanse
of reservoir opens. The runners
sweep onto the ice and gather
around a bonfire built half a mile
from shore. As they join hands and sing
favorite old hymns—"Rock of Ages,"
"The Old Rugged Cross"—I return
to my car, relieved that so stark
an exercise should terminate
with such innocent use of fire.

FEAR TO TREAD

Steven Michaels

Felix stood at the edge of the cliff. *This would be a terrible place to die,* he thought. Nevertheless, he took an outward step and began his descent.

His eyes remained closed. The wind swept all around him. He remained conscious as one does jumping out of an airplane. So few ever consider the implications of a flying leap. Felix could certainly feel the force of gravity. He sensed the nearness of the great stone structure as it seemingly moved upward while he careened rather neatly in the opposite direction.

Down, down, he went. The great mouth of the sea lay open, dotted only with a few protruding rock teeth, preparing to munch upon his body and swallow him up with briny saliva.

Yes. This would be a terrible place to die … if not for Felix's wings.

***

At about five hundred feet, Felix extended his unique appendages outward and glided over the ocean's disappointed maw. For over 7,968 years, he never tired of dropping from great heights. Having lived among humans for so long, it was easy to relish such a death defying skill. Not that he could die, for he was immortal after all. In fact, it wasn't just the thrill of cliff diving that pleased him. It was also the reassurance that his wings could hold him, keep him aloft. Yes, Felix was most fortunate to have wings: a gift from God, quite literally.

Or so he thought…

***

Approximately seven minutes (Earth time) after his descent, Felix received a summons. It wasn't Gabriel, if that's who you're thinking; more likely it was one of his assistants, who was most likely transferred over from Michael's office two millennia ago. Either way, this being was young insofar as celestial types go and she lacked all manner of tact.

"Agent Felix…" she squeaked. She was probably one of those types that could fit on the head of a pin. "I'm Serphina, third order of—"

"I'm aware of you, or at least where you came from," grumbled Felix. "What is it you want?"

"You have been—"

"Summoned? I thought so. Why do we insist on such formalities when we can all see at least seven minutes into the future? Very well! Where to?"

Seraphina was not at all used to this cantankerous attitude coming from a supposedly angelic entity. She smiled politely, but it was obvious she was completely taken aback by him. Felix relished a bit in that.

Damn turn of the twentieth century millennials.

"If you'd be so kind as to follow me, I will—"

"Very well. Fine! Lead the way…"

Travelling at the speed of light, they almost instantaneously arrived in the Alps. Actually, 9,000 feet above the Alps to be precise. And to Felix's surprise, as it hadn't taken them any time to get there, neither Gabriel nor Michael were awaiting them, but rather Raphael (another archangel, not the painter or fictional turtle, in case you are keeping track).

"Sorry to disturb you, Felix," he said as Seraphina and Felix phased into existence on the Earth plane. "Was he at all snarky with you, miss?"

"Well, perhaps—"

"Don't make her feel as though she has a personal stake in this, Raphael," snapped Felix. "Just tell me what's going on, although it's becoming abundantly clear due to our mutual clairvoyance."

"Right. I apologize, Miss Seraphina. You may go now."

She immediately vanished after giving a curt nod to her superior.

"She has quite a bit of potential, you know, which you'd see, if you weren't such an ageist. I was hoping you'd have been kinder to her, but then again, that hasn't happened in 4,000 years."

"Are you trying to insult me, Raphael?" inquired Felix.

"No, merely stating an observation. Isn't that our job, Felix, to observe and intervene as necessary?"

"Ugh, drop the formality. You're as stuffy as your namesake…"

"The painter? Huh, I rather likened myself to the ninja turtle," said Raphael.

"If either one of us is similar to that cartoon character, I believe it would be me," huffed Felix. "Can we just get on to talking about Timothy Langstrom? Nearly seven minutes have passed and I'm beginning to see that's the real reason for all this."

"Very well. Timothy Langstrom died twenty three hours, thirty three minutes, and fourteen seconds ago. I believe he was in your charge."

"Believe?" Felix questioned in outrage. "You know damn well he was one of my clients. Is that term we use now? And what's with being called Agent Felix? Who am I, Sean Connery?"

"Honestly, you couldn't have referenced Daniel Craig or Idris Alba? As I suspected, you are falling far behind the times," sighed Raphael.

"Now who's being ageist?" bellowed Felix.

"Don't be too upset," reassured Raphael, only Felix knew this was all part of their training. In fact, there was a pamphlet drafted over 5,000 years ago called "How to Speak with Other Entities in a Non-Threatening and Angelic Manner." It was, of course, complete bullshit.

"Please don't pontificate with me, just because we're all on high!" groaned Felix. He had had enough. Sadly, the moving finger had already been writ, and he knew what was going to happen next—all clairvoyance aside, in fact.

"Very well. Your trial will commence shortly. Do you have someone for your defense?" inquired Raphael.

"Uh, sure, Max, will do," muttered Felix.

"Max? You mean that lazy fat cherub, who we imported when the Greeks fell? The one that claimed he served Dionysus?" laughed Raphael, dropping all pretense and quickly realizing his mistake.

"Yes, *that* lazy fat ass, you hypocritical, hierarchical toadie! God, why couldn't I have been berated by Gabriel? At least he knows how to play a horn!"

***

In the next instant, Felix found himself surrounded by a cloud bank—and yes, it *was* as cliche as it sounds. Max, wearing a toga with gold embroidery materialized to his right. Raphael appeared to have taken a step towards the prosecution side, if you will, but he was not in charge. No, that privilege fell to archangel Uriel. Known for his poetry, he was an eloquent speaker, and thus a rather overdramatic lawyer.

Zarius, a being who Felix knew through brief encounters with some Hebrew-Egyptian linkage, presided as bailiff.

"Please inexorably rise," he declared while simultaneously manifesting into view. "The Honorable, St. Peter, presiding."

Upon these words, all the heavenly bodies assembled and floated approximately seven inches above the cloud-like plane. And yes, it was *that* St. Peter.

"Felix Unia Aloma, you stand trial for the negligence of guardianship and involuntary manslaughter," Peter began. "How do you plead?"

"Not guilty, your Honor," spoke Max, who knew his client very well but peered into the future just to be sure.

"Very well. As we all knew it might come to this, let it be known, we have a plea of not guilty. Zarius, please swear in the Jury."

"Please raise your right hand and fold back your wings," said Zarius addressing a shimmering hoard that represented a collection of angels that were supposedly Felix's peers, which Felix doubted they were. "Do you solemnly swear or affirm that you will truly listen to this case and render a true verdict and a fair sentence as to this defendant?"

An ethereal buzzing proved their assent and Zarius asked them to please hover imperceptibly for the remainder of the trial.

"Uriel, by representing the prosecution, you may proceed with the opening statement," declared Peter.

"Thank you, your Honor. Cherubs and Seraphim of the jury, we have with us today a veteran guardian angel by the name of Felix. His early record shows an outstanding record as caregiver and protector of those we call mortals. However, in the last 900 hundred years, his performance has been lacking, resulting in near fatal human losses and the blatant disregard for one Timothy Langstrom age 46, who died February 25, 2020 in a skiing 'accident' in the Swiss Alps while on vacation with his family."

"Your honor, I object," declared Max.

"Grounds?" asked Peter.

"The term 'blatant disregard' seems a rather obtuse remark regarding opening statements. We are here to argue that my client has remained dutiful throughout his tenure."

"Sustained. Jury, please ignore that last statement. Uriel, you may continue."

"Very well, your Honor. Regardless of what has been said, we are here today to examine Felix's involvement in the life of Timothy Langstrom, whose human life *could* have been saved by the defendant's intervention, as is the duty of any and all guardian angels."

There was a brief and deliberate pause by Uriel to let this sink in with the assemblage, despite the obvious reasons for this trail. But Uriel, as has been noted, did have a flair for the dramatic, as indicated by his flaming sword which he carried with him at all times.

"Defense. Please begin your opening remarks."

"Yes, your Honor. Although my client Felix hasn't had the best track record of late, we can't place the death of Timothy Langstrom solely on the winged appendages of this guardian angel. If that were the case, trials like this would be commonplace, and it has been at least 400 years since we were placed in a similar situation. As such, we need to examine the events that transpired during the course of Tim Langstrom's life to prove whether or not my client was truly negligent and whether or not he could have done more, although it is unlikely, to change the outcome of the mortal's life."

"Prosecution, you may call your first witness to the stand," said Peter.

"We call to the stand, Timothy Langstrom," said Uriel.

Now because Timothy Langstrom was recently deceased, his body was rather discorporated. Fortunately, 24 hours postmortem gave him some substance, enough to be questioned. And perhaps you're thinking that under the circumstances, these beings should push off a trial, so the key witness could provide more (pardon the pun) substantial evidence. But these beings weren't overly concerned with the newness of a person's death. In fact, calling the deceased as a witness was really just a courtesy extended by the heavenly hosts after Socrates argued in favor of the soul, and more significantly, when Christ got involved as a social worker for all humanity. In fact, in Abraham's time proceedings like this were often settled out of court, what with the voice of God asking people to sacrifice their sons, which was later described as a bad interfaith connection due to a down cosmic server. Ultimately, everyone involved knew the system was flawed, and the irony was not lost on any of the divine beings who created it.

"Witness, will you please remain as tangible as possible and do you swear to tell the whole truth albeit limited by your non-divine senses, so help you God?"

"Urm, sure," slurred Tim, who again, really had no idea what was happening while parts of him kept flickering in and out of existence like an Edison bulb. But again, a courtesy is still a courtesy.

"Mr. Langstrom," began Uriel. "You recently were made aware that you are now deceased; is that correct?"

"Yeah, but I had hoped I was still in a coma, guess I should let go of that idea, huh?" he murmured.

"Yes, sadly, you can," replied Uriel sweetly. "Anyhow, were you also aware of the existence of a guardian angel sworn to protect you?"

"Um, like what my Auntie told me when I was eight? Sure, I guess so."

"And can you identify that being in this near non-existent plane?" inquired Uriel.

"No, can't say that I can," he breathed lazily or would have if his lungs were still a part of his new form.

"No further questions, your honor."

"Defense you may cross-examine," said Peter.

"Thank you, your Honor."

Max was indeed an expatriate from the Greek Pantheon. When it became clear that drunken orgies were no longer tolerated by major religions, he really didn't see the point any more. So he filed for angelic servitude, but mostly maintained harps and looked after sacred wine as befitting his previous work experience.

"Hello, Tim. May I call you Tim?" he began. Is it possible you don't recognize your guardian because only in rare instances did you ever accept such divine interventions regarding your existence?"

"Objection!" declared Uriel.

"Grounds?" said Peter.

"The witness is at best an agnostic, and as decided in the case of Nietzsche, even if God is dead to him, whether he willfully chooses to see or not see divine intervention is irrelevant."

"Sustained."

"Fine. Are you truly an agnostic?" said Max addressing the witness.

"I'm sorry; I was a finance major, and I never bothered much with world religions."

"Very well, so do you believe in any higher power or spiritual guide?"

"I worked at TGIFridays when I was in college, does that count?"

Max shook his head in disappointment.

"No further questions, your Honor."

"Mr. Langstrom you may step down."

"From what? I don't even have toes," sighed Tim, then vanished in a puff of smoke.

"Prosecution, you may call your second witness."

"Thank you, your Honor. I now call Ezekiel Yodder to the stand.

Ezekiel Yodder was an Amish farmer who died in 1811 or maybe 2011; it's hard to know what century those folks are living in. Naturally, he had no problem being sworn in due to his spiritual fortitude being exceedingly strong.

"Mr. Yodder, please tell the court your affiliation with the accused," said Uriel.

"Well, I believe he was what some people call a steward of God and perhaps his presence was often felt in my community."

"This could be promising," whispered Max to Felix.

"But I could not say for sure if that being over there was the sole protector of me and my family. For although he may be an agent of God, it is God almighty who safeguards me from all evils in the material world. Amen."

"Damn," uttered Max.

"No further questions, your Honor."

"Defense. Your witness."

"Mr. Yodder, I stand before you today an ephemeral being, beyond the capabilities of one like you, despite you being well-versed in the bible. I can quote scripture to you, regarding judgment and whatnot, but I won't, because my question is this: how many barn raising did you attend while you were alive?"

"Nearly 45, I should say," beamed Mr. Yodder, proudly.

"And were you or anyone you knew ever injured during one of these?" asked Max.

"No, praise be to God, that never happened."

"And do you believe other forces or agents of God could have aided in these miracles of miracles?"

"Yea, certainly because we are a large community, and although God is great, many individuals, both human and spiritual, help to maintain everyone's safety and well-being. Any Amish will tell you that."

"No further questions, your honor."

"Mr. Yodder, you may step down. Does the prosecution have any more witnesses to call to the stand?"

"No, your Honor."

"Defense?"

"Yes, we would like to call Timothy Langstrom's grandfather, Burt Langstrom, to the stand," declared Max.

Burt Langstrom had died in 1984 when his grandson Tim was only ten years old. It was hard on Tim, despite Burt having led a full life which aided him in a successful transition onto his next plane of existence. Having been dead nearly thirty years made it less challenging to swear him in. And although he still wavered in and out existence on the stand, everyone smiled genially at him, even when his left side dematerialized partly through the proceedings and there was a gaping hole in his torso. Interestingly enough, none of this was due to a death wound he received in his other life, but the fact that sometimes the area closest to the human heart is the most difficult to maintain in any form of existence.

"Mr. Langstrom," began Max. "You died in 1984, yes?"

"Oh yes, I believe they said it was heart failure, but doesn't that apply to nearly everyone in my previous condition?" Burt chuckled; he really was a sweet guy.

"And you visited your grandson Timothy shortly thereafter?" asked Max.

"Yes, I guess you could say it was my one phone call," Burt smiled.

A jubilant buzz emitted from the near imperceptible jury area.

"And did you make your presence known to Timothy?"

"No, sir, I couldn't or at least I didn't know how at the time, but that character over there, he was sort of hovering nearby."

"And what would you say was this being's relationship with your grandson?" asked Max, pointedly.

"Well, hell—oops, can I say that up here?" he blushed.

"It's frowned upon, but we'll allow it," said Peter.

"I suppose then that this fella was Tim's guardian angel."

"No further questions. Your witness."

"Mr. Langstrom, did this being, which the court recognizes as Felix, say anything to you during your visitation?" asked Uriel.

"No, but he looked mighty sad and he shook his head a lot."

"And why do you think he did this?"

"I suppose it was because there wasn't anything he could do for my grandson," sighed Burt.

"Wasn't anything he *could* do or *wouldn't* do?" asked Uriel, coolly.

"Um, I don't know; I really don't know anything when it comes to how this all works."

"Let me put it this way: do you think Felix could have exercised some power during Tim's grieving crisis following your death?"

"Like what exactly?" asked Burt, truly uncertain of these heavenly going-ons.

"Unfortunately, Mr. Langstrom, I can't provide you with examples, for fear of leading you as a witness. So I'll ask again: in your option what is something Felix could have done to or for Tim at the time of your visit?"

"Well, as I said I dunno, but he was there, just the same, and maybe that's enough. There wasn't anything I could do either, but I felt I had to be there and I imagine Mr. Felix did too."

At this statement, Felix blinked hard or would have, if he had actual eyelids, although some argue, in certain forms he had eleven eyelids, but that's not important. Deep down, Felix didn't know if he was ever really doing a good enough job. It was tricky looking after humans. They were so fragile, and it wasn't very clear how often he should intervene or save lives. The reality was he had lots of humans to look after and not just one. He could be in seven different places at once, but it never seemed like that did the trick. But hearing these words: that sometimes just showing up in all seven places at once, a miracle in and of itself, was really the key to all of this.

"Mr. Langstrom, you should be privy to the fact that Tim died nearly twenty four hours ago in a skiing accident, and there is evidence that Felix was not on the scene," said Uriel in the next moment. "With that in mind, should he have been there and should he have stopped the accident from happening?"

"Well, it does seem like an open and shut case, don't it?" breathed Burt.

"No further—"

"But," said Burt loudly. "My grandson wasn't always a daredevil. In fact, I was worried he'd completely shut down after I died. He was depressed. Didn't want to go to school or do much living for nearly two years. Then one day as I understand it, a book fell down off the shelf. Now I'm not sure if it was Felix's doing, but that book inspired Tim to start living again. And well, he learned to take risks, and I believe he knew what he was getting into when he went skiing. I know Tim didn't believe in things like I did, but he didn't have to. When I went to visit him, I just wanted to make sure he was happy, and in a few years, I was really grateful that he didn't keep spiraling. So I'm glad someone was looking out for him."

"But, do you believe it was the being called Felix who supported Tim?"

"I have no evidence to the contrary as he was one of the first angelic beings I met, aside from my case manager, so I'm inclined to think he was doing his job at the time."

"No further questions, your honor…"

"Amazing, Max! How did you find Burt?" whispered Felix.

"He's a simple man, Felix, and he once owned a vineyard, so I got my connections."

"Defense, as we're all cosmically connected, would you please refrain from whispering your asides," quietly berated Peter.

"Sorry, your Honor, old habit from that stint I had in that monastery during the 14th century," apologized Max.

Peter nodded, "Are there further witnesses from the defense?"

"Yes, I would like to call Felix Unia Aloma to the stand."

Again, there was no courtroom drama in response to this, as everyone knew this was forthcoming and not what humans would call a huge revelation. Moreso, Felix was sworn in with ease.

"Felix. Felix. Felix," breathed Max with more confidence than usual. "It has been stated you are a veteran in the divine forces. As such, I think it is clear you have been around humans for a very long time, even by our standards. My question is: are you happy with your job?"

"There are days, well, centuries perhaps. It's not all bad," resigned Felix.

"And when your clients do pass on as it were, how do you feel?" asked Max.

"Terrible, I suppose, but we're not often allowed to feel that way. We know their existence is fleeting, and it is our job to maintain it as best we can and oversee transitions."

"Quite, right. But you said, you feel terrible. Do you think all angels feel terrible as the result of a loss?"

"Isn't that why it rains?" smirked Felix.

A buzzing, something akin to laughter, arose from the jury.

"Please answer the question," said Peter.

"Right, well, I suppose most do. At least the ones who actually care and don't just pretend to do so…"

"But your performance sometimes shows a lack of caring? Care to refute that?"

"You know as well as I do, I worked alongside several Existentialists over the years. I tried desperately to convince them of some meaning, but what was the point?"

"So you uphold that life is meaningless?"

"Some human life, I suppose."

"When you have these thoughts, do you slack off in your job?" asked Max.

"Not intentionally," said Felix, although he was uncertain.

"Why then do you slack off?" asked Max.

"I guess I feel overwhelmed. I know I'm somewhat infinite, but I am not of a higher order. I'm not in command of the heavens like some of you. Do you realize it's been 3,000 years since I visited the Throne and not, mind you, by invitation?"

"Would you care to clarify what bearing this has on your current job performance?" asked Max.

"You know as well as I do, Max, that we're not like them," said Felix gesturing to Uriel and Raphael. "I'm a guardian angel, nothing more! Essentially, a glorified babysitter! And you're a lowly harp maker."

"I take it then you are most dissatisfied with your work. So do you regret not being there for Timothy Langstrom in his hour of need?" asked Max.

"Yes, but no. Secretly, Tim may have had a deathwish."

At this the jury buzzing became like that of actually hornets, angry and appalled.

"Oh, don't give me that!" snapped Felix. "You know quite a few of them down there that have a deathwish! Just ask Unalia who planted the seed for suicide hotlines."

"Excellent point, Felix. I dare say you could have defended yourself and left me to the wine. No further questions."

"Prosecution. Your witness."

"I'm going to get right to the point based on the evidence we have. Let's assume you did nudge the book off the shelf that brought Timothy out of his shell. Are you then responsible for instilling said deathwish upon him?"

"No, he was suicidal upon learning his grandfather died. And I had nothing to do with protecting his grandfather. It was clear he was slated to die. You can look that up."

"Yes, I suppose we could. But did you or did you not nudge Timothy into being a risk taker?"

"I think it could be argued it was the book," said Felix, annoyed.

"And what was the title of this book?"

I honestly don't remember. I read the first page, it sounded intriguing. I was at my wits end, if I had wits, do we have wits? Nevermind, the point is being a guardian angel to a preteen boy is bloody difficult. Hell, nobody gives whatshisname this much grief for waiting until Christ was 33 to set him up for near failure!"

The buzzing then really grew indignant, such that Peter had to call for order.

"Fine," said Uriel. "We shall concede that the job is not easy, but angels are made of sterner stuff than mortals and have been entrusted with the sacred duty of protecting."

"Sterner stuff?" scoffed Felix. "We're hardly on a physical enough plane to be talking like that! So don't lecture me because you inspired several humans to do great things, and by extension, making it seem like angels were bound for even greater things!"

"I am not the one on trial here," said Uriel.

"No, nor would you ever be because you *like* your job. You got the flame and the spear! I was given a harp, or what passes for a harp these days! What's the deal with that?"

"Your Honor, may the witness be asked to step down?" urged

Max. "He's really crushing my own aspirations here."

"He will step down when the prosecution is done cross examining him," decreed Peter.

"Thank you, Your Honor," said Uriel. "Felix, it isn't that you didn't do a good job in the beginning, it's that lately you have not exemplified the virtues of us, the heavenly multitude, regardless of your station. Let me ask you: where were you at the time of Timothy's death?"

"I was atop the cliffs of Moher," said Felix.

"And records here seem to indicate that your entire state of being was there. Can you explain why?"

"I was cliff diving," said Felix. "A sensation that I enjoy only when I am whole and not divided spiritually."

The buzz was quiet but not amused.

"Ah. So despite your ability to be in multiple places at once, you chose to remain intact to dabble in a purely self-serving experience, and by mortal standards, a dangerous practice. This combined with your poor job performance does not bode well for you. And I think it is clear you don't truly value a fragile existence which is the precept of being a guardian angel. I have no further questions, your Honor."

"We will now take a brief recess," said St. Peter. "Now, for the final statements. Prosecution may proceed when ready." (Keep in mind "a brief recess" for infinite beings is sometimes less than a nanosecond).

"Cherubs and Seraphim of the jury, I think much of what transpired here shows that Felix Unia Aloma is guilty of negligence and involuntary manslaughter. Despite the rather dramatic turn of events, which I concede was fun on my part, let me remind you that his infraction is a misdemeanor among our people, and he will not be cast out for any length of time. We're not demons, after all! Therefore, please find the defendant guilty. The prosecution rests."

Then it was Max's turn. In truth, his eloquence and confidence was wearing off, probably because the sacred wine he drank before the trial was leaving his system. However, he did his best to summarize how dutiful Felix had been over the centuries and how important he had been in Timothy's life, despite him being wholly unfelt by Timothy Langstrom. He also concluded that the testimony of Burt Langstrom was truly significant and that the very basic role of any guardian angel is to be there in a mortal's hour of need, and accidents happen to believers and non-believers alike. In fact, if Felix were guilty of anything it was simply not knowing how to work past the limitations of his station.

Then Peter spoke: "Members of the jury, you have heard all of the testimony concerning this case. It is now up to you to determine the facts. You and you alone, are the judges of the fact. Once you decide what facts the evidence proves, you must then apply the law as I give it to you to the facts as you find them. You may now transcend to another plane to deliberate and bring back your verdict."

And just seven minutes before they reached their verdict, the jury returned.

"Have you reached your verdict?" asked Peter.

A ruddy faced cherub materialized out of the ether and spoke as the foreman: "We have your Honor. We, the jury, find the defendant Not Guilty."

Felix was relieved. Had he been found guilty, he would not have relished going on probation and separating himself from the Earth for 2,000 years. In fact, Earth was the one thing he liked about his job. He was always amazed at what a gifted artist the Almighty was, especially in His prime before humans went and loused a great deal of it up. Either way, the trial was just the push Felix needed. He was readily able to acknowledge his mistakes, and he humbly begged for forgiveness; he was in heaven after all, and it felt as though it had been granted to him. Moreover, he vowed to do a better job, especially for Timothy's son, to whom he was made a guardian, and who, oddly enough, was also named Felix. And with any luck, he hoped his new client might take up motorbiking, something Felix always found fascinating...

THE BLUE LIGHT

Shonna Ryan

As a writer, I have always been of the opinion that any good love story has to start at the very beginning. I have come to believe that for the reader to really be convinced of the romance in the story, they must also fall in love with the object of the main character's affection. This is only plausible if the object of affection captures the reader from the very start; that first glance, the first kiss. This personally held opinion has made it nearly impossible for me to write short stories due to my obsession with cataloging the romantic progression of my characters.

However, this is not a love story, and it is not about two fictionalized characters. This is a true story that I can only categorize as a tale of horror, and for me it is personal. It is the story of my husband's apparent dissolution into madness, and the ultimate discovery that it was not madness at all, but a truth far more terrifying.

I will refrain from my propensity for unnecessary backstory; you don't need to know about how I met my husband in college, or about our drunken first kiss in the back seat of a minivan, or about our wedding on a hot July afternoon. What you do need to know about is our home, because this is the setting of the tale that I am about to tell.

After finishing graduate school, we were lucky to happen upon a year-round cottage available for rent in the woodland setting of Westport, Massachusetts. Unlike most of Massachusetts, which is largely comprised of suburban homes compressed upon each other,

Westport retained a certain bucolic charm; acres upon acres of farmlands rolling along gentle hills and melting into a briney river that leads out to the Atlantic. It was a score to find a two bedroom cottage built at the turn of the 20th century that we could actually afford on the piss poor salaries of recent grads who had just built up a mountain of college debt.

Upon moving in we furnished our beloved rental with second hand furniture bought from antique emporiums in nearby New Bedford. We became diligent with developing vegetable gardens during the warm seasons, and learned to live with frigid floor boards in the cold months. For five years this little cottage was our home, and it was here that we cooked many good meals in our impossibly small kitchen, watched sunsets transpire with ice cold beers in hand, and made love with the shades wide open at nights, with only the stars as witnesses. For five years everything was lovely aside from the occasional blizzard or other such natural conflicts that arise when one lives in fairly close proximity with that bitch Mother Nature.

Actually, that is not entirely true. For five years everything seemed normal, or at least some close proximity to normal. On the weekdays we were your typical pleasant married couple; we woke up and brewed coffee and packed lunches and kissed goodbye before parting our separate ways down the dirt road in route to work. On weekends there were smokey charcoal BBQs, occasional parties, and many whiskey laden conversations. When the mood struck, perhaps there was the occasional dabble into psychotropic drugs. It is only in the interest of complete honesty I mention the drugs, since as the story progresses you may wonder if chemical influence was involved.

Therefore, I must underscore that it was very rare circumstances under which such things were imbibed.

In any event, as I said, most things in our life were quite normal. Although, there were certain aspects of living in the woods that created a slight tension from time-to-time. At first I thought of this as quite normal since we were both city born and raised. It seemed only natural that our foray into a home without neighbors, surrounded only by trees and all manner of wildlife, inflamed certain anxieties at times. Perhaps it was the outcome of watching too many horror movies, or perhaps it was just the legitimate fear of knowing that if you screamed nobody would hear you. Whatever it was, the nights were hard for us to adjust to at first. It was just a bit too quiet. Then the night terrors started. We didn't think much of them at first. We had both been restless sleepers since childhood. What was there to do but laugh off the screams that woke us from dreams we could never quite remember afterwards.

Shortly after moving into the house, my husband developed a bit of passion for UFOlogy, which is to say the study of Unidentified Flying Objects. There was nothing unusual about this in and of itself. We both loved the television show, X-Files. It was no surprise, given that my husband had majored in Physics, that all things space related were of great interest to him. It began with YouTube videos that he would often show me at the dinner table. Then it evolved into the reading of more prominent theories from other sources. I got a bit wrapped up in it myself.

At bedtime, we would lay in the dark, willing sleep to come join us in our marijuana induced haze. The next day promised to be another long work day, so sleep we must, yet that made these stolen moments all the more golden. Our room enveloped us in pitch dark and silent except for the soft vocal tones of George Noory interviewing some exuberant man about his alien abductions. Occasionally, the sound of one of us savoring the final sips from a tallboy of Guinness added to the ambiance.

As I listened, I wondered what it was like to absolutely believe in the paranormal, the supernatural, and the extraterrestrial. I wondered what it was like to fully know that there was more to life than the stagnant repetition of the day-to-day; more than the observable prison of survival. "I want to believe," I spoke to the darkness one night, grinning at the nostalgic joy brought to me by the X-Files quote.

"I do believe" he responded from his side of the bed. "I have to believe. I'm a scientist, I know of infinity."

These musings about there being more to the universe were nothing of concern to me at the time. In fact, it elated me most often. Nobody wants to be alone, nobody wants to believe the universe is an icy and vast nothingness, that we are here by mistake, without meaning or purpose. Then there came a conversation one morning that tilted the trajectory of things in such an unperceivable way that while I could not have possibly known it at that time, I would later wish I had fled that cottage right at that very moment.

We were fishing on the river that morning, in that grey hour just before the sun rises when the fish are more apt to bite. We stood at the edge of the dock with our poles cast out into the dark water, and he spoke suddenly of a strange memory. "When I was a kid, we were driving back from vacation in Canada and we lost time."

"Lost time?" I yawned, imagining this was some expression I was still too dull to suss out.

"It's like what they talk about often in UFOlogy. People describe suddenly losing time. One minute they're doing something super ordinary and it's, say noon, and then time seems to skip and it's suddenly 4:00 p.m. and they have no memory of where the past four hours went."

"I drank a whole bottle of Jameson once and lost eight hours" I jested, but he barely cracked a smile, and I realized this was rather serious to him.

"We were driving back from Canada, and it was a little past midnight. I was about twelve years old. My Dad was at the wheel, my mom in the passenger seat, and I was wide awake trying to beat Pokemon Red. I remember my Dad saying 'we need to get gas' in this tired voice, and I realized the time. Then, suddenly, it was 3:02 in the morning. I still had my game in my hand, and we were still on the road, but we weren't moving. My Dad kinda eased on the gas, like he wasn't sure why we stopped. Maybe he thought we'd run dry, but the gas gauge was at the exact same spot it had been.

My dad said, 'what's wrong with the clock?' and my Mom looked at her watch. 'Mine also says 3:02,' she said, and we just kept driving.

But I could see something in my dad's eyes in the rearview mirror; like a sort of panic. We all knew something was wrong, but somehow we just couldn't be sure."

I stared at my husband through the murky light and knew his words would go on to haunt me for a long time: "*We all knew something was wrong, but somehow we just couldn't be sure."*

He continued, "My mom finally mentioned it years later, after my old man passed away. She said they talked about it many times after the fact, and they just couldn't fathom where those three hours disappeared to."

"So, do you think … do you think your family was abducted?" I asked without being patronizing. "I've already told you part of me always wanted to believe, I just lack the quantifiable research to make it real to me. I'm pragmatic like that."

"I don't know, but there have been a lot of weird things that have happened to me and all my family members over the years, things I sort of shrugged off. But when I started learning more about UFOlogy, a lot of it matches up. Lost time, weird markings that appear on the body overnight, waking up in odd locations with no memory of moving. It's all so easy to explain away. With my brother we'd say, 'oh, he sleep walks', or when that unusual mark appeared on my mom's neck, we worried about cancer, but it was nothing the doctor could explain. But now I wonder … I just … wonder."

I bit my lip and had no response but to reel my fishing line in and try to recast while my mind mulled over what he had just said. He was certainly right; it was all very easy to explain away. The fact that his story matched up to those he read about online didn't mean jack shit. It's natural to seek paranormal explanations for the perfectly reasonable; it makes us feel special or important somehow. Still, his story sent a chill down my spine that I couldn't shake off. *"We all knew something was wrong, but somehow we just couldn't be sure."*

It was shortly after that when I started noticing the blue lights.

Actually, I think I may have been seeing them for a long time before that, but didn't consciously remember. I lose many nights of sleep now wondering just WHEN exactly I did start seeing the blue lights.

The first night I remember seeing them was during one of my many evenings of restless sleep. Insomnia has always been an on and off struggle for me, but unlike some insomniacs, I long gave up wandering the house or any of that nonsense. I force myself to lay in bed and work through the plot details of whatever I am writing until I fall asleep. This is the only tactic I've ever found to combat insomnia. It only works 10% of the time, but any insomniac will tell you that those are odds worth taking. Anyways, I laid there wide awake, and I recalled my husband's story and wondered if I could wrap that into my latest attempt at fiction as he snored blissfully beside me.

Then it happened; a blue light flashed into the room so bright that I thought a lightning bolt must have struck in extreme proximity. The last thing I recall thinking is "What the hell…" then I woke up the next morning. I could not remember any dreams, which for me is very peculiar. Aside from the night terrors, I can typically recall every dream I have in vivid detail—much to the annoyance of friends and family, who never really want to hear about my stupid dreams.

While this certainly struck me as odd, it wasn't anything to "write home about" as they say. Then the same thing happened the next night. So on the third night, I was inspired to stay the hell awake. After my husband fell asleep that night, I sat up against the headboard and fixed my eyes on the window across from the bed with fierce determination. I felt fairly certain I wouldn't actually see the stupid light, but then, just as before, the flash occurred and I told myself,

"Stay awake … get up … go to the window…" But everything faded, and it was morning again.

I didn't say anything about this to my husband. Not because I was particularly scared; after all, what was there to be scared about? I saw a blue light, and then I fell into a deep sleep. Unsettling perhaps, but not exactly the stuff of horror movies. Besides, after a couple weeks had passed, I didn't see the blue lights anymore. No, the reason I didn't tell him was because his interest in UFOlogy had grown into a full blown obsession and it was becoming concerningly unhealthy. In my pragmatism, I imagined that his dissatisfaction with his current occupation was causing him to seek further meaning and purpose, not from the bible, but from the cosmos. I figured that he wanted, no needed, to believe that the strange occurrence with his parents on their trip from Canada meant that his family was special in some way. That he thought they had been selected to be studied by extraterrestrials because they were unique somehow. While such a bizarre belief was concerning to me, it wasn't the worst thing I could conceive. His discontentment could have led to an affair, or worse yet, born again Christendom. Still, I didn't want to feed his delusions with my weird blue light story.

However, as with all poorly kept secrets, things intensified over time. I began to notice that in the middle of the night he would no longer be in the bed with me. When I would look for him, I'd find him standing in some corner of the house, naked expect the boxers he'd fallen asleep in. I convinced myself that work-related stress had led him sleepwalking, but part of me knew by this point that I was the one being foolish. I felt like Scully from X-Files; I had seen the evidence, but I still refused to believe.

He said nothing more to me about aliens or UFOlogy, but he would retreat into our small study whenever possible to feed his obsession by the pale glow of the computer monitor. Then, one day, he appeared before me in such a sudden and startling way that I nearly dropped the stack of papers I had brought home to grade.

"What do you make of this?" he asked me, presenting his forearm. At first, I thought he had just lost his mind. I began to consider what resources were available to thirty year old men who had cracked under work stress. Then I saw what he was referring to; five dots in a perfect line along the soft flesh of his forearm. They were tiny but perfectly shaped, in a shade of black so inky that I thought he might have made them himself with a pen. But as I wiped at the dots, I could feel something under his skin, like tiny braille bumps. I retracted my hand with the same intense speed with which he had appeared. After over ten years together I can honestly admit that I was quite familiar with that man's body down to the very freckle, but I had never seen these markings before.

"You should go to a doctor," I suggested in a shaky voice.

"Yeah, I suppose you're right," he said in a dull tone, and that very moment I just knew there was no possibility of that happening. I wish I had told him right then about the blue lights, but what good would it have done?

That night, when we went to sleep, I made every effort to stay awake and see what might be happening to my husband in those dark hours, in the woods, in a house void of neighbors, with only stars as witnesses. But that ended up being the last time I ever saw the blue light, or my husband.

GAS STATION TIME MACHINE

Chele Pedersen Smith

Gas light! Ugh. Of course the imp would mock me when I was lost in the dark without a cell signal. My classic, lime-green Gremlin could last at least twenty miles, but in the pitch black the road seemed endless. If only I could focus on road signs, but none blipped by. Dread and worry jitter-jattered my brain. How many miles was it til the next town?

Up ahead, the reflective strips of a guard rail curved, so I followed it. But yikes, it was a hairpin turn! I hit the brake and spun, clenching my jaw—and steering wheel—as the car slid down an embankment. Thumping tires bounced us into a blind pit as leafy overhangs slapped past. At last the vehicle rolled to a halt through thick pines—just a smidge away from a looming sign. The larger-than-life words caught in the high beams gave me chills: Welcome to Massachusetts.

In the dead of night, the sign was anything but welcoming. But then I saw one even worse: "Berkshire Mountains. Bear crossing." Great! Insecurity swept my stomach. I longed to be anywhere but here. But where was I exactly, besides on the brink of one state and the smidge of another?

Against the swelling moon, distant birch brambles curled like the crooked hands of witches. Hoots spooked the air. Fighting off tears and a frightening intuition, I peeled out, stepping on the pedal in reverse. But my wheels spun, stuck in a rut.

I already had one scare tonight. After dropping Cousin Janie off in Troy, New York, I headed east into the night toward home. Every so often, a jangling from my hatchback bothered me. Every few minutes, I couldn't resist peering past my shoulder to check. I knew what the ruckus was, but alone in the massive midnight abyss, it rattled my nerves. On my last look-see, I noticed flashing police lights so I pulled over.

"Good evening, miss. License, insurance, and registration, please. You were weaving a bit back there. Been drinking?"

"No, sir. It's just … my turntable clanking."

My excuse was so lame, even I didn't believe it, but pointing his penlight into the back, he indeed found the stereo culprit.

He handed my documents back. "Alright, keep your eyes on the road. And have a good night."

"I will, thanks." He started to step away. "Oh, officer. Do you happen to know where the nearest gas station is?"

He hesitated. "Um, sure, about five miles down. Then turn right. It's hardly a town, so don't blink. Good night … uh, Gigi," he smiled.

Caught off guard, I returned the grin. That's when I noticed he was sort of cute, in a limited light kind of way. I eyed his name tag. "Thank you, Officer Carson."

I drove on, hopeful, more relaxed. But … how the heck did he know my name? Then it hit me: *your driver's license, dummy*! Right … but it only revealed my real name, Georgette. I mulled the mystery over for a bit then started daydreaming, hypnotized by the reflective barriers. That was how I found myself face-to-face with the *Welcome to Masshole* monstrosity, and I decided to brave the wildlife to see why my car wouldn't budge.

Stepping out, an owl shrieked! I dropped my phone, then caught it, my knees shaking just as much as its roving illumination. When the shine hit the side door, I burst into giggles. One puzzle was solved—my deejay services magnet, Gigi's Gigs! *Clever eye, Officer Carson.* I needed one too as I scanned the undercarriage, then scrambled inside, pressing 9-1-1. To my amazement, it connected!

"Hi, a big tree limb is jammed under my car." Based on my Google map pin, I gave the dispatcher clues the best I could then thanked her.

It was a chilly wait, so I huddled into my hoodie. An imaginary scenario with a certain officer entertained my brain. Within ten minutes, a patrol car pulled up. Nerves pounded my chest. Would it be my cute cop?

The policeman approached, carrying a blinding light. "Ma'am, you okay?"

Squinting, I rolled down the glass. Tall, dark, and handsome, but not him. Drats!

"I'm Officer Zenda. You look distressed."

"Oh … it's just that my car is stuck."

"You're okay now. Towing will arrive shortly," Zenda assured. "Where are you heading?"

"Well, I was supposed to take an exit for gas."

High-pitched beeping punctuated our conversation as a tow truck backed up. Twisting around, I saw another squad car.

When the second officer checked in, my heart raced. Then, the name tag hit the serotonin jackpot.

"Officer Carson, remember me?" I rushed in one breath. "The stereo girl …"

"Ah, yes," he chuckled. "But this doesn't look like a filling station, Gigi."

"I know. Not having the greatest night," I sighed. "Don't even know how I got here."

"Gigi, like the musical?" Zenda cut in. "That's my favorite."

"Hey, my wife's too," Carson said.

My heart sank like a stone in Lake Onota.

Zenda snapped his fingers, aiming one at me. "'Diamonds are a girl's best friend, right?"

"Oh, well yes, the song in the show. Not for me, personally."

"Nice, a girl of simple means," Carson nodded.

To my surprise, he offered his hand as I rose from the car. Our fingers zinged! Minutes ago we could've run off to Maui, but now that he was married, my imaginary game was no longer fun.

However, my amusement peaked watching my rescuers. As if wrestling a gator, Zenda and Carson jostled the tree limb free. With the crane hooked to my bumper, my car followed suit. A round of applause broke out.

"Thank you so much!" I gushed to them all.

"Good luck. Get home safely," Zenda nodded. He left, following the truck. In the dark deadlines of two states, it was just me and Carson caught in his strobing squad lights.

"We have to stop meeting like this," I joked.

"Agreed. Wow, didn't mean to sound cold." He reached out

about to pat my shoulder but let his arm drop instead. "I just meant ..."

"I know. I'd love to be off the road and in bed right now."

He bit his lip to hide amusement, folding his arms as the ruby reflection swirled across his cheeks.

"Oh, I didn't mean it like that," I laughed. This time it was more than the siren coloring *my* face. "Just want to curl up with a book under my comfy covers."

Carson chuckled. "Tell you what; I'll escort you to the gas station. Then I'll know you found it, and you can be on your way safe and sound ... and in bed," he winked.

As I followed his lead, my heart fluttered thinking how gallant he was. *Silly, the dude is hitched!* I squeezed the steering wheel firmer.

He pulled into a one-stop convenience and coffee shop near a rundown service pit. Above the two-sided gas tank were a double row of lights. One was burned out, the other on intermittent life support. The neon sign omitted some letters as well.

Instead of announcing what I guessed was Optimal Fuel & Donuts, the remaining lit characters spelled TIME OUT. Awesome! I was ready to take a break from this awful night. Just needed to fill up and high tail it home, but the place didn't exactly look open.

In front of us, our cars' beams revealed a demolished heap of the store's remains. Maybe gallant wasn't the right word.

Carson strolled over and leaned in. "There was a fire on the coffee side about a year ago. Took down the place, but the gas pumps work. Wow, this is a ... curiously cool ride."

"Thanks, family heirloom. Sometimes more trouble than it's worth. Like me," I grinned.

"No trouble at all," he smiled. "You should be all set here. It's a bit eccentric, but Gus is legit."

I looked around. "Oh good. I bet your wife worries overtime with you on the night shift."

"Yeah. Well, she did. It was what we fought about most." He grimaced. "Ex-wife."

"Oh! So sorry." I rested a hand on his elbow, not really sorry at all.

"Thanks, that's kind of you." His warm eyes invited me in like chocolate.

In the fuller light of the flood lamp, his features came into focus. He was no obvious George Clooney, but he had his own brand of subtle attractiveness. Stocky build, tousled but regulation hair, crooked nose. Slight acne, but his scruff covered most of it anyway.

"Not sure what's up. I'm not usually this helpless," I assured.

"Yeah, I rarely come across the same damsel in distress twice in one shift."

"So it happened before?"

"Just once, and it was a blue moon like tonight." He pointed at the lunar glow above. "Second full orb this month."

Mesmerized by the vertical creases when Carson spoke, I nearly reached out and touched them.

Ping! Ping! Ping! The urgent tone of my dashboard's S.O.S snapped me out of my stare. "I better feed this thing. Thanks again."

"Good night, Gigi," he bid with a glint, sliding into his car.

I putted over to the pump. Pulling the lever of my gas cap release, the amplifying pop jolted the silence. I climbed out and couldn't help glancing his way again. He waved. I looked down for a second, embarrassed, but when I returned his gesture, he was gone. I surveyed the area and didn't see taillights in the distance—in any direction!

An electrifying buzz from the only working bulb tasered my trance. *This is no time for love!* The foreboding scene seconded the notion.

I searched for a credit card slot but struck out. Between the establishment's ghost town ambience and old school machinery, I was stranded on a deserted concrete island.

"Cash it is."

Leaving my purse on the console, I dashed over to the dim hut, relieved to find a lumpy man wearing a mechanic's suit stitched with "Gus." I handed him a crumpled five and a tentative smile. He took them with a nod and the emotion of a robot.

Back at the pump, I unleashed the unleaded handle. A flash from the fluorescent rod zapped, crackling like the execution of a dozen moths.

The *ding, ding* of a car tripped the arrival switch. I looked around, hopeful. Had Carson returned? Hmm, no, I was still the only customer. I returned to my task, about to sink the nozzle into the car's tank.

"Good evening! I'm Cal. Full Service, sir?"

I jumped, stifling a scream. A young attendant appeared wearing crisp, blue coveralls and a cabbie cap. With the persona of the teenage boy-next-door, something was off, like he sprang off a too-happy billboard advertising an appliance.

"Excuse me," I corrected, rifling my short, chic hairstyle. "I'm a woman."

"My mistake, miss. Men drive more where I come from." He took the gas hose from me and stuck it into my car's reservoir. "Window wash?"

Cal tapped a squeegee from the soaker and streaked the glass.

"Hold on, where *are* you from? Because women drive as much as men."

"True, ladies do drive, but like I said, most of my customers are men, especially since the second war ended."

He was back to fueling the car, clicking the handle to assure a proper fill-up.

"Okaaay ... but watch it. I only gave Gus five bucks. I can't pay if it goes over."

"Then you're in luck, miss. You'll be due plenty of change."

"Whaaat?" I shot a look over at the kiosk, now brightly lit. Was it my imagination or was the outline a much younger, thinner Gus?

To the left, the fragrance of fried decadents rose from the shop. The wafting lured me sideways. I floated over, suddenly starved. Odd, moments ago it was a pile of rubble.

Over on pump island, the abrupt beat of bubblegum music bounced between the speakers. I smiled at the catchy song, "Sugar, Sugar," by the Archies. I be-bopped over as my favorite roller rink record whisked me away to simpler times. Funny, both beams of fluorescent rods burned brand sparkly new.

Reaching into my car, I whipped out my cell phone. God, it was after one o'clock!

Cal jumped in front of me. "Hey, hey, put that away. Don't you know cells blow up gas pumps?"

"That's just a myth," I dismissed. "It was busted years ago."

Cal's scowl unnerved me. I followed his glare and saw the gas pump begin to smolder! I tossed the phone on the passenger seat like it had the plague.

The arrival ding tripped again. This time a convoy of Cadillacs roared in, leaving a chorus line of others down the road.

The speakers blared a Benny Goodman swing tune.

Out on the street, Caddies without headlights passed a few modern vehicles who flashed theirs as a courtesy.

"Oh no," Cal groaned. "Here we go again."

The rat-a-tat of machine guns pierced the air, shooting the signalers. Cal grabbed my hand. "Run for cover."

We ducked behind the attendant's booth.

"Oh my god! Why did they do that?" I asked.

"Gang initiations."

"Pretty harsh!" I sputtered.

"Haven't you ever read chain letters?" Cal scolded.

"Chain letters?"

"Don't tell me you never received notes of caution or money schemes through the U.S. Postal Service. And you better have mailed them out to the two people listed on the letter or you'd have bad luck for years."

"Oh those emails? They're just urban legends," I snorted. "And so '90s! They're social media memes now. Like, beware of hundred-dollar bills stuck on windshields at the mall—carjackers plant them to lure shoppers out of their cars? Ha! Those messages are just mass hysteria spreaders, so no, I don't forward. I delete them."

"Bad juju," Cal clicked his tongue. "Sure you want to risk it?"

"Yeah, I think I'm good. Besides, I'm pretty sure the headlight hoax meant urban gangs, not prohibition gangsters."

A scuffling of wingtip dress shoes scraped the gravel behind us. "Oh yeah, doll face," a goodfella sneered. "Wanna bet a bootleg on it?"

The scorching scent of freshly fired sulfur burned my nostrils as two mobsters cocked Colt pistols at the side of our heads.

The boss grabbed my arm and another dragged Cal, marching us over to the convenience store. We landed beside an ATM that looked like it came through the apocalypse.

"Work the voodoo and give us the dough," Boss Man ordered.

"I-I don't have my bank card. It's useless without it," I trembled. Was this really happening?

"Cut the mumbo-jumbo." The thug pressed the gun against my spine.

Then Cal whispered, "Plug your pin in backward. It'll call the cops."

Oooh, why didn't I think of that? Oh yeah, because I didn't believe in these things. "Without the card, would it even work?" I whispered back.

Cal shrugged.

With nothing to lose, except maybe our lives, I tapped my personal identification number in reverse.

The goons vanished.

Cal and I exhaled, venturing outside.

"Where'd they go?" Scanning the area, the Cadillacs were gone.

We ran back to the pump. "That was close," I told Cal, leaning against my hatchback.

"See, better safe than sorry."

I barely had time to register the fright when a shadow approached, and a sheet of paper smothered my face. "Perfume sample, lady?"

I ducked, but not before the whiff invaded my nostrils. To my surprise, it was pleasant. "Oh, lilac. My fav—"

Dizziness spun me into Cal's arms.

"Gosh, I tried to warn you." Cal's voice seemed to echo through a faraway tunnel.

The next thing I knew, I woke up drenched. "Oh no, did it rain? Can this night get any worse?"

Cal held up an empty water bottle. "Sorry, didn't know how else to snap you out of fainting."

"I passed out?"

"I'm afraid so. Just don't sniff any perfume samples again."

"I'll try."

Cal helped me into my vehicle. "Thanks." I relaxed against the headrest and closed my eyes. A ding called Cal away.

A scurrying skimmed between my nose and cheekbone. I froze, suddenly remembering a warning about toilet seat spiders. When I opened my peepers, a woman in a power suit leaned over me, her ombre hair skirting my face. She pressed a business card into my palm with urgency.

"I've heard the whole conspiracy from your virtual phone assistant," she said, crushing my hand. "I'm a government agent and need to take you in for questioning."

The card cut into my flesh. "Ow, government questioning? What conspiracy?"

"Don't deny it. Strange things have been happening tonight, have they not?" When I nodded, she launched into a lecture. "And you're the ringleader; I take it? If you don't confess, I'll have to scan your brain."

"No! I'm a customer. Cal, help! Tell … her. I … had … noth—" My speech slurred in slow motion until I lost the ability to form any words at all. An alarming sensation skulked up my spine. Like being comatose yet conscious.

The next thing I knew, my hand was plunged into a bucket of icy, blue windshield wash. After several swishes, Cal patted my mitt dry with a paper towel, dabbing away any last trace.

A few minutes later, I was able to bat my eyes. Other movements returned slowly.

"Golly, the business card was laced with a nerve drug," Cal said.

"What's … with … all the … loonies on the loose?" I touched my head, still a bit woozy, but at least my speech was returning with quicker cadence.

Then a voice boomed over the loudspeaker, startling me next. "Miss, please come to the booth. Your credit card has declined."

Slinging my bag over my shoulder, I stumbled over.

"I didn't … pay with plastic … Remember? Only cash."

Gus leaned forward and nodded. "I know, lady. But a man climbed into your back seat. I called the police, so just stay put."

"Omigod! Okay … " Of course I liked the idea of a cop showing up.

"Oh wait," I told Gus. "The man in my car is probably Cal."

"Who's Cal," he grumped. "Your boyfriend?"

"No, you know, Cal, your gas pump guy. Cheery chap, shiny cap. He's been helping me all night."

"I haven't hired anyone in decades," the boss gruffed.

I looked around to point him out, but the place was a shambles again. When I glanced at Gus, he was back to his old, dumpy self.

Baffled, I slid into my car. I peered into the back, just in case. All clear! Were the shenanigans over? Clutching my phone, I decided to summon Siri for directions home, but the spy's conspiracy came to mind. Nah, better not chance it. I hoped my sense of direction jived with intuition this time. I snapped on the radio to keep me awake. Perfect! Journey's "Separate Ways" pounded an offbeat path for a welcomed getaway. I sighed relief as the miles ticked away, but before I found the next exit, there were flashing lights behind me again. I wasn't speeding and no stereo swerving this time. In fact, nothing was wrong. Or … could it be *him*? My pulse set off fireworks. I was out of his jurisdiction, so probably not. I started to pull over but suddenly remembered something my dad told me.

"Geeg, be careful," he said. "If you get pulled over, don't stop. There are imposters out there. Drive to a populated area, even better if it's a police station."

At the time, I blew it off. Sounded like another stupid email warning. "Yeah … exactly the kind that is wreaking havoc tonight!" I eyed my rearview mirror. As I looped off the interstate, I saw a twenty-four-hour diner ahead. I parked under the fully lit picture window.

The patrol car squeaked into the space next to me. I looked over, hopeful, but the cop getting out was not Carson. The policeman stood, arms folded, his shorter partner right behind.

Winding my window down, I shouted in one breath, "I didn't pump and run. Cal filled the tank!"

"Okaaay…" The cop named Diaz gleamed his flashlight on my passenger seat. "Who's Cal?"

That was the million-dollar question. "Gas station attendant," I muttered. "Sorry, wasn't eluding you. It's safer here in case of posers and all."

"Perfectly understandable, Ma'am," his partner, Goodwin, cut in with a chipmunk voice. "It's a full moon. Or is it fool moon?" Her laugh tittered like broken glass, adding to the warped night.

"Miss," Diaz continued, glancing at my license. "Someone in your vehicle has been waving to us through the taillights."

"What!?" Chills prickled my spine. I jumped out.

"Mind if we take a look?" Diaz asked.

"Please do!" I bit my thumbnail in suspense.

Poking around, Goodwin chirped, "Just sound equipment."

My blood pressure began its descent. "But how did you see a hand waving?"

Diaz inspected closer. "Ah, a leaf! Must've been flapping." He patted his chest. "My bad. The old eyes playing tricks."

"Too much caffeine," Goodwin sang as they crouched into their cruiser.

I waved to the officers, relieved when their tires crunched in reverse. My hunger returned. I dug through handfuls of loose change in the bottom of my bag and score—most were quarters. "The pastry case is mine!" Dashing inside, I drooled over an array of pies, eclairs, lemon bars, or …

"One French cruller, please," I told the clerk.

The crinkling of tissue paper transferred the treat.

I strolled along the counter, debating whether to eat in or take out when my foot caught the base of a spinning stool. To my embarrassment, of course it was the only occupied seat.

"Pardon," I mumbled, placing my hand on the person's arm to steady myself. To my surprise, a cop looked up. But not any cop. *The cop.*

"Carson," I blushed.

"Hi, Gigi. Amazing, we keep crossing paths." He nodded at my colossal cruller. "Breakfast or after-midnight snack?"

"Both," I chuckled. "Helluva night. You won't believe the mayhem going on at Gus's."

"Oh, I can imagine." He smiled, picking at his pancakes.

"You knew!" Hand on hip, I wasn't sure if I was ticked or amused. "Was this some kind of sick joke? I've been held at gunpoint, nearly robbed, drugged twice for possible kidnapping and who knows what else. Unbelievable. I thought you were one of the good guys."

I stepped away in a huff, but he gently pulled me back. "I *am* a good guy. And truly sorry. You needed gas in a hurry, and it was the closest fill-up. I figured you'd grab and go before the Tom Foolery began."

"You sent me there! I can't believe it."

"Well, there's usually a hero on hand and the incidents are harmless. They're delusions, actually."

"Delusions? Harmless? They sure felt real, especially the gun stabbing my back." Then I frowned. "Hmm, come to think of it, they did poof away once the hoax was carried out. It was like solving riddles in an escape room of horrors—extreme edition."

Carson winced. "Again, very sorry. Luckily, they rarely happen. Only once in a…" He gestured his fork toward the wall.

"Blue Moon Eatery?" I stared in awe at the electric sign.

We shared a laugh.

"So it truly was a night of lunatics!"

"Oh yeah!' He fished his phone from his jacket, flashing the date. "Extra creepy points when midnight morphs into April first."

"What are the odds?" I whistled.

"Right? I think fate's playing a hand tonight." Carson rearranged scrambled eggs on his plate.

"You believe in fate?" I gushed.

His eyes met mine. "I think I do."

My heart fluttered.

"Have a seat," he chuckled. "Coffee? Regular or unleaded …"

"Unleaded," I laughed. "Thanks, Officer Carson."

"Call me Todd. Hey, the Policeman's Ball is looking for a mixmaster MC. Interested?"

I smiled and swiveled in close, curious if I'd get to taste the maple syrup on his lips, wondering if this counted as a date and how he took *his* java du jour. At this rate, I'd probably never get home, but this time I didn't care.

SEASONS

Nancy Barker Sawyer

The flower turned toward the Prince and said,

"Release me from my bed of grass

and cradle me in your hands.

Caress my petals gently with your lips and taste the nectar of my life."

"But if I do so," replied the Prince,

"You shall change.

The secret of your beauty will no longer hold its mystery.

I may not have the magic to keep you fresh and alive.

If you should wither and fade because I held you in my arms,

I would lose all hope for tomorrow.

Please let me admire you from a distance.

There you will be safe from harm,

and I can still call you my own."

"But don't you see?" said the flower.

"My beauty lies only within your eyes.

My life is full because of you.

My fragrance will grow stronger

pressed against your body's warmth."

The Prince smiled and gently released her.

He pressed her to his lips and sighed:

"I shall be your sunshine, rain, and soil

You shall be my strength and comfort.

Together, we will grow until our Season ends."

GPS

Kathy Chencharik

Joe dragged the hunter's dead body beyond the pathway and dumped it. He took the hunter's bow, quiver of arrows, and the GPS before disappearing into the deep woods of North Central Massachusetts. Snow drifted down from a cloudy sky, adding to the eight inches of white stuff that had fallen in recent days. Joe heard the sound of snapping branches, looked up, and noticed a large animal moving among the trees. Placing an arrow into the bow, he pulled back, and sent it flying. As he trudged through the snow, seeking his prey, he tripped over a fallen log. The GPS sailed through the air and vanished into the sea of white. Joe noticed tracks with spots of blood, and he followed the red trail through the snow-covered woods—leading out into an open field.

The wind picked up. Snow mixed with sleet came down at a faster clip, not only covering the blood of the animal he'd shot, but his own footprints as well. Without the GPS to guide him, he headed out across the field. When he reached the other side, he spotted a log cabin nestled in another stand of trees. Smoke curled up from its chimney. Joe headed for the cabin. Climbing the snow-covered stairs that led up to a porch, he stomped the snow off his boots and knocked on the door.

The door opened a crack. An old man with wispy white hair peeked out. "Can I help you?"

"I hope so," Joe said, holding the bow and adjusting the quiver. "This is my first time hunting around here. I was following the tracks of an animal I'd shot when this freak snowstorm took me by surprise. I lost my GPS, the tracks of my prey, and my own tracks as well."

The old man eyed Joe up and down. He opened the door wider. "GPS you say? I believe I've got just what you're looking for."

"That's great," Joe said as he stepped inside. "Where is it?"

"In that room," the old man said, pointing toward a closed door.

Joe followed the frail old man into the darkened room. He glanced down and noticed a bloody arrow lying on a table near the door.

"That arrow belongs to a friend of mine," the old man said, following his gaze. "I can tell by the initials. You're also carrying his bow. And since I know he would never freely give them to anyone, I'm assuming he's dead."

Joe nodded and smiled. His smile soon faded when he heard a low guttural sound coming from the darkest corner of the room. A large white dog, almost as big as a bear, emerged out of the shadows. A blood-soaked bandage was wrapped around its right leg. The dog growled, bared its teeth, and lunged.

"Well, there you go," the old man said, watching as Joe tried to fend off the attack. "Meet my GPS: Great Pyrenees, Samson."

THE CHOSEN GIFT

Sue Moreines

I always dream about being on Broadway, going to the moon, exploring the Alaskan wilderness, hiking the Appalachian trail, climbing to the top of Mount Everest and hundreds of other adventures.

Of course, I don't venture too far from home, since getting around in my wheelchair limits my excursions. I was told I had an accident when I was seven, which paralyzed me from the waist down, but I don't remember it. I also have no memory of life before I became tethered to this chair. Apparently, I loved running, playing tag with my sister Grace, growing carrots, and riding horses, but hard as I try, all I see is a blank screen.

After our parents died, Grace moved away, and I continued to live alone in our farmhouse, looked after by one aid or another. I counted on them for virtually everything and couldn't be more grateful. Reading, writing, daydreaming, watching television, and spending time outside keep me pretty busy, and since I've never known any other life, I've been fairly content.

However, nights are really tough, lying in bed for far too many hours feeling completely constrained. On a positive note, that's when I do the most thinking, focusing on what it might be like to be fully independent.

Every morning, Matt comes into my room, pulls back the curtains and says, "Good morning Nick! Let's get the show on the road!"

I respond with, "Can't you come up with something new to say?"

Then Matt smiles and says, "And ruin my record? I think I'm up to 842, give or take a few hundred."

Matt has always been my favorite assistant. He's only a few years older than me, and taught me a lot about life, but from the perspective of an able-bodied person. I can tell him anything, but I don't, and you don't need to be a therapist to figure out why.

I love the feeling of having control over what I say, since being a paraplegic means having to count on others for so many things. Now, we're not talking about life and death events, but simple activities I prefer to keep to myself. For example, on my daily "rides" outside, I often veer off into the brush and purposely fall out of my chair. It's always exciting and scary to figure out how to get myself back into my carriage without being covered in dirt and leaves, and avoid scrapes and bruises. Matt has questioned me a few times, but I've always convinced him to believe me, even about how a wad of grass found its way into my underwear. He also doesn't know he's the protagonist in the book I'm writing, but I figure I'll let him know once it's published and share the royalties with him.

Yesterday was particularly important, and I'm definitely going to tell everyone about it. It began like any other day...

***

"Good morning Nick! Let's get the show on the road!" Matt

announced.

I said, "Can't you come up with something new to say?"

"And ruin my record? I think I'm up to 843, give or take a few hundred," Matt replied with the updated tally.

Then he asked, "What's your plan for today, Nick?"

"Well, I'm going to drive the tractor out into the far pasture to collect field stones so I can finish rebuilding the wall across from the horse barn," I answered.

After chuckling, Matt said, "Sounds like a lot of physical work! Would you like any help?"

"Of course not! I've done this myself for years, and certainly don't need anyone to get in my way now," I responded, wishing it were true.

"OK, I'm going to run some errands and find something good for dinner tonight," Matt said on his way out.

I watched him drive away and wondered how I would spend the next two hours. Coming up with creative ideas after 30 years isn't easy, but I've always managed to find a way to keep occupied. As I headed down the hall, I stopped in front of the door that led to the attic.

"How is it possible I'd never been up there?" I asked myself aloud.

The answer didn't matter, since I hit the "idea jackpot."

I released the rusty latch and looked up at a steep set of about 20 wooden stairs. Even though I have an extremely strong upper body, I didn't know if I was capable of pulling myself to the top. There was only one way to find out, so I set the brakes on my chair, lowered myself to the ground, and leaned against the stair treads to see if they were solid enough to withstand my weight. They creaked and I groaned as I began the ascent.

I was sweating profusely when I safely landed on the attic floor, and it took a while before I could breathe without gasping for air. My forearms and elbows were covered in blood, and I knew that dark purple bruises weren't far behind.

Fortunately, two small windows allowed in enough light for me to see without need for a flashlight. Good thing, since I didn't have one. A moldy smell permeated the air and everything, including me, was covered in grime. Mouse droppings were scattered about and the floorboards were rough and uneven. I knew I was going to be pulling splinters out of my body for a very long time.

There were a few tattered boxes filled with girl's clothes, an old sewing machine cabinet, a child-sized saddle and one of my dad's hunting rifles tucked into a corner. Nothing Earth-shattering or especially valuable, but then I noticed a shiny brass handle on the back wall. I moved closer to have a better look, and saw that it was attached to an elaborately carved small door.

I stared at the amazing piece of artwork, which depicted an open gate with trees and flowers in the background. I tried to guess who designed it, what might be inside, and why it was here in the first place. I wondered if squirrels or bats were on the other side, but still planned to open it and chance being bitten by a possible resident.

I pulled on the handle and as the door squeaked open, I was immediately blinded by a pulsating light. My entire body was sucked into its core before the door slammed behind me, and I was carried away. Although the sensation was exhilarating, it became terrifying when I heard a whispered voice. At first it was hard to decipher, but soon it became clear, "CHOOSE!"

The voice repeatedly ordered "CHOOSE, CHOOSE A DESTINATION," which increased in volume until the sound became deafening. I wasn't sure where I wanted to go, or how I was supposed to choose the location. Eventually, I just screamed, "STOP HERE!" At that very moment, I was gently dropped to the ground and found myself lying in the grass, looking up at the sun.

Seconds later, I had an out-of-body experience. I watched and listened from above, as a clip from my past played out on a real-life movie screen.

***

"Come on Nick! Tag, you're it!" yelled Grace.

I jumped up and looked around for my sister before calling out, "Where are you?"

"It's your turn to catch me," hollered Grace, from behind the horse barn.

I took off running as fast as I could, tripping and falling once, but never stopping. When I got to the back of the barn Grace wasn't there, but I caught a glimpse of her in the cornfield.

Before I could chase her, Mom called out from her vegetable garden, "Nick! Would you please come help me pull some weeds?"

Looked like Grace would have to wait, which always made her so mad. Mom and I laughed every time we heard her screaming my name.

When we finished, Mom said, "Go get her, Nick!"

I took off running again, only to find Grace scowling as she walked toward me. She gritted her teeth and said, "Leave me alone, Nick. I don't want to play anymore."

"Oh well. Your loss," I replied, and headed to the barn.

"Hey Dad! Want to take the horses out?" I asked.

"Sure! Great idea. Saddle up!" Dad said.

So, I watched myself and Dad ride through the fields and over a hill or two, before having to get home for dinner. Life seemed pretty good back then. In fact, I heard myself say it was the best day ever, just before the horse bucked. I fell backwards into our stone wall, leaving me unconscious and severely injured.

***

I started to come around when I heard my name being called and felt someone touching my shoulder.

Matt was staring at me when I opened my eyes and said, "What the heck are you doing lying here in the grass Nick? You're filthy! And how did your arms get so beat up? I always knew you were up to something when I found prickers on your socks and mud splattered on the back of your chair."

It took time before I realized I was home, and then clearly remembered that I had accidently chosen something miraculous. Having the opportunity to witness life as a physically active and happy little boy was a gift. Seeing the accident play out was quite the opposite, but I finally felt whole, in spite of it.

It was time for me to fess up, so I asked Matt to help me get back into my chair and said, "You're right Matt. Of course, I haven't always been honest with you, but I can't wait to tell you what happened today. It started when I opened the attic door..."

COSMIC SERENDIPITY

Harvey Silverman

Visits from *Beyond*. Séanceal communications with the departed. Pennies from heaven.

Silly.

How comforting to the deluded it must be to believe that the loved one, wrapped in celestial finery, is "okay" and watching over us, ensuring that the intangible thing called love remains requited. How full the grieving heart must feel to see that favorite pet reappear once more as a companionable shape in the clouds. How relieved the heartbroken must be to complete what is thought necessary to release the poor soul trapped in some halfway place on the way to eternal rest.

Foolish. Wishful thinking. My faith resides in facts, in reality, in science.

Still, keep one's mind open. I find agreement with the words of the remarkable polymath, J.B.S. Haldane: "It is my supposition that the Universe is not only queerer than we imagine, it is queerer than we can imagine."

Queerer than we can imagine. Beyond imagination. Wishful thinking is imagination without effort, and it is so easy to fall into its trap.

***

My mom had survived lung cancer 10 years earlier, but her lungs were damaged beyond repair as her overall condition deteriorated. In January 2009, Gretchen and I stopped at her Worcester home to say goodbye as we drove on from our Manchester, NH home to winter in Florida. Short of breath, using supplemental oxygen continuously, stooped and slow moving, my mom's decline frightened me. I hoped I would see her again when we returned in late March.

For 20 years, I had travelled to my folks' Massachusetts home in spring and autumn to spend the day helping my mom in the very labor-intensive task of making her legendary—at least in our extended family—gefilte fish. For the last 10 years, the day included an extra hour—each way—drive with my mom to a kosher market in Connecticut to get the required fish no longer available locally. She had been 69 years old when I judged her *too old* to be making her special dish alone. At age 86, when she had finally found the fish's preparation too difficult even with my help, she still enjoyed a twice-yearly trip to the Connecticut market.

When we returned north at the end of March, 2009, my mom was even worse. There, on a sofa, her head down, her legs so grossly edematous that lymphatic fluid sometimes leaked through her skin, sat my mom. She struggled to stand when I arrived unannounced, a bright smile replacing the dull mask on her face. After hugs, kisses, hand holding and expressions of happiness from each of us, I asked her if she wanted to make our spring trip to the market.

"Of course!" she exclaimed.

Two days later I picked up my now 88-year-old mom. Our time together on the drive to Connecticut was sweet. Unspoken was the understanding that this could be our final trip. Spoken were memories and some stories I had never heard. I asked her if she was afraid of death. She was not. I asked her if she thought she would go to heaven.

"I don't know where I'm going, but I know it will be with your father." He had died the year before.

Two months later my brother called to report, our mom had become acutely ill and was en route to the local ER. I quickly gathered what I needed and left for Worcester, stopping at a local gasoline station to fill my tank. I pulled up to the pump, opened the door and there, on the cement, was a penny. Immediately, before I could manage a single thought, a single idea, a single reaction, my dad was in my mind. A sign that he was with me, with us. A penny from heaven.

Wishful thinking. A random event given supernatural significance. Simple coincidence.

My mom died in June, less than a month later. A few more odd episodes in the next months were likewise examples of wishful thinking. The skeptic that I am recognized how easily one can ascribe significance to chance occurrences, perhaps subconsciously seeking them and attributing meaning to them when none exists.

In early November, 2009, Gretchen and I left New Hampshire for our Florida winter. It was a lovely day, clear and sunny, making for an easy drive. As usual my mind wandered here and there. Nearing Hartford, I realized this was the first time I had driven on this road since that sweet trip with my mom half a year before. I said nothing to Gretchen but smiled at the memory and recalled silently the happiness of that time. I continued the reverie as we drove on.

And there, on the exit ramp, was a truck with a company name in large letters on its side:

HARVEY

My name! Just another and perhaps more dramatic example of wishful thinking. But what was the chance that at that moment, on that day, when I was lost in thought about my mom and our trips, a truck with my name would be at that very spot?

I suppose that is the definition of coincidence.

***

Friendship, dear and deep, is a wonderful gift of life. My good fortune includes two irreplaceable lifelong friends.

When I later recounted to Carl the sighting of my name on the truck and the totality of the circumstance, his reaction was immediate and straightforward. There was nothing of significance, no greater meaning. He termed it *cosmic serendipity*.

Carl was a college classmate, smart, stubborn, hardworking, fun-loving. He was given to excess and at times might tend toward the ostentatious; a part of his personality that, rather than off-putting, added to the enjoyment of being with him.

His death, not unexpected, occurred at age 70 in 2016. Our trip to his memorial gathering in December was a challenge; after flying across the country, we had to drive 200 miles through a sudden and unanticipated blizzard. The hardship of travel was simply accepted; it is what one does to honor the memory of such a friend.

A few days later as we drove our rental car toward the airport, returning home, the memorial concluded, the goodbyes to those he left behind heartfelt, the overcast sky gave way intermittently to bits of sunshine, the drizzle slowing at times but never ceasing. A rainbow appeared, came closer, and suddenly the car was filled with rainbow, sparkling colors inside the car, the windshield ablaze as if one resided within a prism, the color spectrum full. Seconds later, all was gone.

A random confluence of moisture and sunlight had occurred at the moment we drove on that particular stretch of highway. A strange coincidence, ostentatiously excessive.

***

Uncle Jack, my mom's older brother, was more than my favorite uncle; he was a member of our household during the years I grew up until I left home for college. He had his own bedroom, shared the bathroom. I saw him daily. We are all unique, of course, but some it seems are more unique, further down the unique bell-shaped curve, than others. Such was Uncle Jack. Odd in a pleasing way.

After I left home, my folks downsized and Uncle Jack moved into his single occupancy apartment. He remained a part of family gatherings, and it was always good to see him over the years as I became an adult, married, and had my own family. The warmth between us was understated and enduring; to me he was more than an uncle and to him I am certain I was more than a nephew.

He died in 2004 at the age of 87. He owned little; I kept an oversized cardigan sweater he rarely wore, my younger brother kept a hat and a couple of other items. I enjoyed wearing that sweater on cold New England mornings as I drank my coffee and read the morning paper.

I wrote an affectionate remembrance of Uncle Jack several years after his death which was eventually available in print and online. The morning after Christmas, 2016, was the first day the essay became available. My brother, who was visiting for the holiday, and I were in the kitchen. He had just read the essay, enjoyed it and the memories it generated, and we were talking about Uncle Jack.

I noticed a bit of trash on the kitchen floor. I bent to pick it up to throw it away. It was a name tag, the sort that might be sewn into clothes. The name on it was Uncle Jack's. Where had it come from? The sweater I had worn hundreds of times over the years? My brother had brought nothing with him of Uncle Jack's. Why was it found on the same day my story of Uncle Jack had been published?

An odd coincidence. Odd.

***

When I told my remaining irreplaceable friend the story of the rainbow we agreed it was inexplicable and left it at that. What more was there to say?

Dave was a sensitive, kind, and empathetic person but inept when it came to some simple tasks. His friends often did things, unbidden, that seemed to be too much for him; hanging a window blind, setting up his stereo, defrosting his freezer.

A friendship that began at age six had naturally over the years created not merely its own history, stories, memories, but certain traditions, customs that almost became ritual, repeated year after year.

For decades, I had called Dave on his November birthday to wish him a happy day. He usually tried to do the same for my May birthday but almost always was a day or three early or late. He would call and with excitement in his voice wish me happy birthday, sometimes telling me, "I nailed it this year!"

"No, Dave. Sorry, it was two days ago, but thanks anyway." Or perhaps, "Thanks, but you're early. Not until tomorrow."

Dave's brother was several years older and so off with his own friends when Dave and I were growing up; I hardly ever saw him. He was already married and living an adult life while Dave and I were still in college. I had spoken with Jim a literal handful of times over the years; the most recent nearly 20 years earlier at the funeral of their father.

In January, 2018, Dave became suddenly and severely ill. From afar, I learned of his illness and intractable comatose state a day before Jim called me. Dave's doctors had advised Jim the situation was hopeless and that life supportive measures should be withdrawn. Jim knew I was a physician, albeit retired, and asked for guidance. It was a weekend so I suggested he wait until Monday and review the situation; nothing would change, I knew, but my unspoken thought was that waiting a day or two would make any feelings of guilt Jim might feel for *pulling the plug* less likely.

Dave died the following day thereby relieving Jim of the responsibility of making the decision. At Dave's funeral Jim and I spoke amiably, said our goodbyes, and I left expecting I would likely never see or speak with him again.

A few months later I unexpectedly received a call from Jim

who wondered what specialty of physician he should see for a certain medical question. I gave him my best advice, and we chatted for a few minutes about Dave. He chuckled once about something or other and for just that moment he sounded exactly like Dave; it was if I were listening to my old buddy. The moment passed, I did not remark upon it. After I hung up, Gretchen pointed out that it was my birthday, and I had been called by Dave's closest relative. Jim did not know it was my birthday but when it came to the date he had indeed "nailed it!"

***

Coincidence. Episodes of wishful thinking. Cosmic serendipity. Perhaps.

NEVER FORGET ME

Diane Kane

I opened my heart to the empty room. At first, it gave no sound. Then, I heard a faint creak from near the bed. My body froze while my thoughts raced. Bloodstains still splatter the rose trellis wallpaper just as I had seen in the faded newspaper pictures from years ago.

Tiny hairs on my arms rose as I stood in the frigid air of the old house where my biological parents once lived, and I was created. I ran my fingers along the faded oak dresser.

"Who am I?" I wondered aloud.

It was no secret that I was adopted as a newborn. However, I'd never been told where I came from until I turned 18. My adoptive parents sat me down. With anxious eyes, they handed me an envelope. It held several cutout news articles that told a dark story of my beginning. I made a note of the address stated in the report. After several weeks, I finally found the nerve to search for my forgotten past.

"Who's here?" I asked my stark surroundings. It answered with a faint mumble. I had come to the abandoned Victorian mansion in search of the ghosts of my past. I hadn't thought it would give them up so easily.

Dust began to dance in the old bedroom. Particles sparkled with life. The icy cold air that had enveloped me a moment earlier was gone, replaced by a warm, gentle embrace. I stood transfixed in its mist.

Police Called to Domestic Dispute, the headline had read.

The air around me grew heavier—harder to breathe—like a weight on my body. Reaching out, I felt its substance in my hands. Then I saw it, just as if it had always been there. Gray, grainy molecules pulsed with electricity. The particles fused into an orb of energy that grew until it almost filled the room. There was warmth in its touch, safety in its pressure, hope in its existence.

I closed my eyes. The image of old newsprint mirrored on the inside of my lids ... *husband in a fit of drunken rage* ...

For a moment, I thought about running. Then the feeling passed. I extended both arms towards the ceiling; my hands cut through the gray air as if it were fluid. The substance clung tight to my body yet let me turn freely, with resistance not unlike water.

Pregnant female rushed to the hospital with multiple stab wounds...
My mind stirred with a noise, unlike I'd ever heard. The symphony of sounds, soft and loud at the same time, inhabited my head. It was impossible to describe with adjectives—sounds of existence, joy, love, creation—not made for human ears. While severed sentences continued to echo in my subconscious

Husband takes his own life...

Standing wide-eyed in disbelief, I looked around in desperate need of someone ... a witness to my encounter. Then, a calm came over me. This wasn't a random phenomenon. I belonged here— just me—alone. Had I found what I'd been searching for?

While mother clings to life...

I turned in a complete circle to find the aura surrounded me in a vast sphere. Within the area, the fuzzy gray air blurred my vision, but

I could look beyond the distortion. About three feet out in all directions, I could see the end of the apparition. Outside the circle, everything remained in perfect clarity.

Infant delivered by Caesarian section

Walking towards the edge of the circle, I stuck my arm through the perimeter. I could see goosebumps on my flesh in the stark, cold air. Quickly, I pulled my chilled limb back into the warm density of my circle.

"Do you know me?" I asked.

Still disbelieving my senses, I sought to test the limits of the apparition. Reluctantly, I stepped outside the circle. My body shivered with the chill. I turned in fear. My protective sphere was still there, pulsing and sparkling. I ran back to its embrace. It wrapped around me, just as I had never left.

Mother succumbs to wounds … Infant survives.

Words whispered in the empty room as the air cleared, "Don't forget me."

"Never," I promised.

BEYOND THE PATHWAY

Karen Traub

Ghosts are real. They appear in the form of memories, deeds, and items left behind. Spirits of people who lived before reveal themselves to those who are receptive. Untold stories and unresolved mysteries linger and haunt. They can also inspire. Acts of kindness and generosity are not always lost to future generations. Real or imagined, the spirit of those who lived before can change the course of our lives.

I feel the present slip away as I enter the old town hall. Sunlight filtering through the big wavy windows illuminates dust motes, disturbed and dancing. The one-story wood building smells of old papers and the dampness that creeps in over time. It is quiet here, in a way that my life usually is not. The spacious solemnity of this old building makes it feel like a church.

A regular Tuesday morning in the spring of 2005. Husband at work, kids at school. As a library trustee, I am tasked with making a list of items that belong to the library but are stored here at the old town hall. Town clerk Leslie Bracebridge is helping me. The M.N. Spear Memorial Library in Shutesbury, MA, was built in 1902, still has no running water and is so small that for every new book acquired, an existing book must be removed. The library's 1902 annual report boasted an increase of the collection from one thousand to twenty-five hundred books. Today, there are over 10,000 items in that same space—including books, CDs, DVDs, and audiobooks.

I write the titles and authors of books that remain from the library's original collection but are now stored here, including *The American Frugal Housewife* by Mrs. Child 1832, *History of the Connecticut Valley Ma with Illustrations* 1879, and *The Underground Railroad in Mass* by William Siebert 1936. Leslie points out some other items. I write on my yellow legal pad "a bookcase, a portrait of William Spear (in need of repair), and a large antique table with crystal ball feet."

While I take notes, Leslie bustles around, emptying the dehumidifier and commenting on the constant battle against mold. She turns the metal wheel and opens the great black door to the town vault.

"C'mon in," she ushers me, after assuring me that it's impossible to get locked in. I follow her into this realm of treasured town memories.

Next thing I know, I am holding the ledger containing the names of the first patrons of the public library. I feel overwhelmed, unqualified to be holding such a precious artifact. Seeing the names of the first library trustees, William Hemenway, Newton Crossman, and the first librarian, Miss Mary Clark, people who nurtured the seeds of the library and helped it grow, I feel the responsibility of carrying their work forward.

It is cool and claustrophobic in the vault. There are metal shelves that are nearly empty and on one shelf there are several leather bound ledgers. Beside the ledgers there is a little wooden box.

"Go ahead," says Leslie, "open it." I do. Here in my hands is a message from the past which at this moment is mine alone to open.

Tentatively, I open the box. Inside are square scraps of fabric that could be for a quilt, a thimble, and a small photograph in a gilded frame of a young girl with a serious face and straight dark hair. I lift them out. Underneath, at the bottom of the box, folded in squares on soft paper, a note which begins "Dear Lucy," and ends "your friend, Laura Berry."

Shutesbury, Mass

March 4, 1892

Dear Lucy:

It wasn't so that Dearie could come over to see you today after all, as the wind blows and she has the head-ache too.

She says tell you she is going to be an old lady a while longer and will come over some other day to play with you.

Have you got your bank full of dimes yet? If it isn't send word to me and Mary and I will (each) give you one.

Am sorry you are sick, hope you will be better soon. I am coming over to see you some day. Bessie sends her picture to Charlie. I wish you had one for us. I must close this letter now so good-bye.

Your friend,

Laura Berry

This box was left here, among the items belonging to the library for a reason. But why? I am determined to know who these people were and why this box is here. But I have work to do now. I read as much as I can of the ledgers. We stay until it's time for me to pick up the boys at school.

Back outside, the robins bob and peck for worms as Leslie and I walk back across the spongy green common to the town hall. I feel hungry, tired, and exhilarated. Black-capped chickadees call from across the street. A blue jay squawks. I am so full of impressions, ideas, and questions that I can't think of a word to say. Leslie is similarly quiet.

The letter, folded neatly and small enough to fit into the little sewing box, impresses me as being particularly kind and encouraging, as though from an older neighbor or cousin.

Who was Laura Berry? I feel an affinity for her. I even like her name. Who was Lucy and did she get better? And Dearie? Was that a person or maybe a little dog? I knew I had to find out as much as I could.

Over the next few years, I filled in some of the blanks by researching birth, marriage, and death records. I found myself becoming the storyteller as well as a part of the story.

I learned that little Lucy Hamilton, aged six, died of diabetes three weeks after the letter was written in March of 1892. Laura Berry was a library trustee and the daughter of George Berry who was a selectman, overseer of the poor, and one of the wealthiest men in Shutesbury in the late 19th century. He died in 1910.

In the early 1900s, the plan for a reservoir meant the Swift River Valley was to be flooded. The four towns of Dana, Enfield, Greenwich, and Prescott were unincorporated, the people displaced, and even the dead were moved. I learned that a large portion of Shutesbury's most fertile farmland in the valley of the West Branch of the Swift River was also sacrificed for the creation of the Quabbin Reservoir which, combined with Wachusett reservoir, still provides Boston with 200 million gallons of water every day.

Laura Berry taught at the schoolhouse down the road from her family's home on land that was taken as part of the Quabbin watershed.

I recently visited the Berry homestead, located at the end of the road that leads to the water. Gnarly sugar maples, rambling lilacs, and scattered daylilies among the stone walls and crumbling foundations are all that's left in the part of town where the Berrys and other prosperous families lived and worked the land.

On this tree-lined dirt road where there are no houses, cars, telephone poles, or other signs of modern life, it feels possible that I could meet Laura Berry. Two time travelers, Laura Berry and I, sat among the wild raspberries, blueberries, ferns, moss, oaks, and birches.

I stand a moment, watching the sun move toward the tops of the trees in the west. Listening with an open heart, wondering if her spirit visits this place. Wondering what brought me here. What have I learned? What would I ask her? What would she ask me? I feel that the best we can be is to be remembered. I want to remember her.

Laura Berry was a library trustee in the early twentieth century when the library was new and prospects looked bright. I was a library trustee at the beginning of the twenty-first century.

I live in an extraordinary time of global pandemic, social upheaval, war, technological expansion. So did Laura Berry. The beautiful valley where Laura Berry's family came from, lived, and were buried, is now flooded. Gone. What is not under water has returned to wilderness.

If we lived during the same time, I imagine Laura Berry and I might have been friends.

Beyond the pathway, ghosts exist to urge us to go forward without forgetting the past. Beyond the pathway we're free to remember, to explore, and to dream.

OUR CONTRIBUTORS

ABOUT OUR FOUNDER

Steven Michaels is the author of *Sweet Life of Mystery*, a parody of the whodunit genre. He has been featured on The Satirist website for his scintillating take on current affairs, and has written, produced, and directed over twenty plays for students at Winchester School in New Hampshire. Steve founded the Quabbin Quills in 2017 and was instrumental in creating the first anthology, *Time's Reservoir* and he hopes you have enjoyed the work he has featured in all of Quabbin Quills' anthologies. He is also very thankful to all the authors who have come to share his writer's dream.

ABOUT OUR PUBLISHER

Garrett Zecker is the publisher and co-founder of Quabbin Quills. He holds an MA in English from Fitchburg State University and an MFA in Fiction from Southern New Hampshire University's Mountainview MFA. He founded Perpetual Imagination in 2004, specializing in independent releases and live events. Garrett is a writer, actor, and teacher of writing and literature. Links to his work, including other publications, full Shakespeare In The Park performances, and hundreds of book and movie reviews can be found at his blog: *GarrettZecker.com*.

ABOUT OUR EDITORS

David Barry is a psychotherapist who writes genre fiction. He hails from Worcester, Massachusetts, where he spends his leisure time with his life partner, her daughter, their dog Lola, and a cat named Mouse. You can follow David (and Lola) on Twitter at @DavidMBarry.

Ruth DeAmicis has finally retired from working as a journalist for too many years and has set her sights on fiction and poetry. The notebooks and scraps are coalescing as we speak, and a new fantasy novel is 50 % there!

Cecilia Januszewski is a sophomore at Reed College, where she's majoring in Linguistic Anthropology. She is proud to be the secretary of Quabbin Quills and has been published in several anthologies, and is currently in the process of finishing her first novel. In the future she hopes to attend graduate school for Linguistics, but in the meantime she's staying busy baking, dancing, and rewatching Scooby Doo.

Diane Kane dabbles in all genres and explores every aspect of writing and publishing. She measures her success by the friends she has made along the way. You can find her work in numerous anthologies, magazines, and periodicals. Her love of writing led her to be one of the founding members of Quabbin Quill's non-profit writers group. Diane is the publisher and coauthor of *Flash in the Can Number One* and *Number Two*, stories to read wherever you go. She writes public interest articles for Uniquely Quabbin Magazine and professional reviews for Readers' Favorite. Her recently released children's book *Don Gateau the Three-Legged Cat of Seborga* is published in English, Spanish, French and Italian. Look for her latest children's book, *Brayden the Brave* available in book stores and online.

Charlotte Taylor has published short stories and poetry and hoards a collection of unedited novels. She loves the process of creating characters, stories, and worlds. Charlotte is an active blogger for her work in Ayurveda and yoga. She is actively seeking a life of peace, study, and fun. Charlotte can often be found surrounded by cats with a mug of tea and reading books. Other times, you'll find her practicing yoga, climbing mountains, and sometimes crawling under barbed wire.

James Thibeault is proud to be one of the executive board members for Quabbin Quills. He has two published novels, *Deacon's Folly* and *Michael's Black Dress*.

Karen Traub is a member of the Quabbin Quills editorial board and Straw Dog Writers Guild and is a '21 graduate of the Newport MFA at Salve Regina University. Her poetry and prose appear in *Voices of the Valley* and *Beyond the Pathway* anthologies, *Brevity, Multiplicity* magazines and she writes regularly for several publications on *Medium*. Karen lives in the Swift River Valley of Western Mass with her husband Frank and her Royal Python Chloe. Follow her on: instagram.com/happydancermom/

Michael Young is the current Poet Laureate for Royalston, MA. His work has appeared in three former Quabbin Quills anthologies as well as *Uniquely Quabbin Magazine, Trout, Grit,* and *A Time for Singing*. Currently he is working on his memoir, *Playing in the Weeds*. As a proud Adult Ed. instructor in creative writing at MWCC (The Mount), two of his students have pieces in *Beyond the Pathway*. Michael enjoys fly fishing when not writing or working with his wife, Pat, on their Greenfyre Farm. His weekly Universal Meditation show may be heard on WVAO-FM.

ABOUT OUR SCHOLARSHIP RECIPIENTS

Katelyn Stolberg
3rd Place: Pause
Katelyn Stolberg is originally from central Massachusetts but now lives in Boston, MA. She is a combined B.A./M.S. degree student in Behavioral Biology with a minor in Autism Spectrum Disorder (B.A.) and Biology (M.S.) student at Boston University. In her free time, her passions include writing, painting, and exploring the city. Katelyn's poetry has been published in other anthologies as well as on various online platforms; her titles include "Lying Flat," "Dear Little Girl," and "Broken Record."

Jillian Mawaka
2nd Place: Bird Lady
Jillian is a senior at Minnechaug Regional High School and has always had a passion for writing. In tenth grade, she was awarded the Outstanding Sophomore English Student Award by the English department. She has been writing poetry and stories since she was very young,and enjoys writing about her own personal experiences.

Violet Masterson
1st Place: Check, Love
Violet has no other published work to her credit, but she has written countless short fiction pieces in her spare time. As a junior in high school, she has taken three English classes and two creative writing classes.

ABOUT OUR CONTRIBUTORS

Jonathan Bishop's work has appeared in a variety of outlets, including *Laurel Magazine, Burning House Press, Culture Cargo Cult, Melbourne Culture Corner, Fourth & Sycamore, Boston Literary Magazine, The Arts Fuse,* and *Write City Magazine.* His first collection of poetry, *Scratching Lottery Tickets on a Street Corner,* was published in 2018 by Finishing Line Press. He has appeared in the previous two Quabbin Quills anthologies. He is a founding co-editor of *Portrait of New England,* a literary journal, and a co-founder of *The JT Lit Review,* a blog.

Kathy Chencharik lives near the Millers River in the North Quabbin area. Her poetry, non-fiction, and fiction have appeared in several newspapers, magazines, and anthologies. She won the Derringer Award for best flash fiction for "The Book Signing" in *Thin Ice* (a Level Best Books anthology, 2010). She earned numerous honorable mentions for her stories in Alfred Hitchcock's Mystery Magazine's *Mysterious Photograph Contest.* And her story "The Widow" was *"The Story That Won"* in the November/December 2020 issue of the magazine.

Les Clark grew up in Boston, having five jobs before entering the Air Force and five jobs since. Les should be retired, but there is still so much to do, like finishing his fourth book. Les has been writing since the elementary stewards of his education demanded to know what he did last summer. Les still works in retail, where he meets the cast of characters he often puts into his writing. Les has degrees from Northeastern in Business Administration. He applied those skills in a business he ran for 26 years. Les gives credit for his writing to his high school senior year English teacher ("Clark, what is this?") and Stephen King, who advises him to write every day.

Phyllis Cochran retired early from a career in business and became a freelance inspirational writer. Her work has appeared in *Chicken Soup for the Soul* books, *Woman's World, Grit, Focus on the Family*, and various magazines as well as several anthologies. She has taught Writing for Publication and Memoir classes. Her book *Shades of Light –A Spiritual Memoir* was published in 2006.

A New England native, **Virginia Davis** divides her time between writing and clothing/accessory design. Her fiction has been published in the Los Angeles-based literary journal *Delphinium, Alm* magazine and *The Blotter* among others. She lives in Portsmouth, NH.

William Doreski lives in Peterborough, New Hampshire. His most recent book of poetry is *Mist in Their Eyes* (2021). He has published three critical studies, including Robert Lowell's *Shifting Colors*. His essays, poetry, fiction, and reviews have appeared in many journals.

Allan Fournier is a retired software engineer who has always enjoyed working with words, including poems about family, New England sports championships (they've kept him busy!), musical artists, and various "themes" at local open mic nights. He recently published a poem titled "Thank You COVID-19?" in a local library's COVID anthology.
Notes about his Poems: "Ain't No Mountain High Enough" *is about a literal "pathway" up Mt. Washington, then the virtual "pathway" his sister was inspired to take to become a New Hampshire "peak bagger" to raise funds for fighting Parkinson's disease, then another literal "pathway" to complete her last peak with family and friends.* "Crystal Lake" *is about all the detours during a family vacation "pathway." Yes, it is a true story.*

Jeanne D. Gilbert was a Rehoboth correspondent for the Attleboro Sun Chronicle in Massachusetts for 17 years. She also owned and operated Gilbert's B&B for 36 years. Moreover, she has raised, trained and showed horses throughout New England for many years. She has been married to Donald Beardsworth for 14 years. She enjoys spending time with her three adult children (and spouses) and eight grandchildren and Don's three adult children (and spouses), five grandchildren and four great grandchildren.

John Grey is an Australian poet, US resident, recently published in *Orbis, Dalhousie Review* and *Connecticut River Review*. His latest book, *Leaves On Pages* is available through Amazon.

Sharon A. Harmon a freelance writer and poet, has two chapbooks of poetry. Most recently, she has had a story included in *Chicken Soup* entitled, "Christmas is in the Air." Sharon has taught workshops on poetry and writing for magazines. She is also the author of the picture book, *Horatio Mortimer Loved Music*. Sharon is currently working on writing and illustrating her second children's picture book, *Francois Christmas Crossing* for the Fall of 2021.

Cathy Carlton Hews has recently published a memoir about her time caring for a parent with Alzheimer's, titled *A Bagful of Kittens Headed to the Lake*. One of her essays, "I'm Seeing a Bunch of Bitches Later", won an honorable mention in the *Writer's Digest* annual writing contest. She has written for *Stage Raw*, a Los Angeles theatre website. She also had a weekly column "Backstage with the Betty" Eye Spy LA, from 2005 to 2007 in addition to a column "Betty, Please," Salon City, a national arts- & culture magazine distributed by Time Warner, February 2007-2009. She is currently living in western Massachusetts and working on her second book, *Invisible Woman*.

Maggie Nerz Iribarne is a lifelong writer, happiest with a blank journal and a pen in hand. Aside from writing, she loves her husband, son, and working as a tutor at Le Moyne College. She practices her craft on the third-floor attic of her home in Syracuse, New York. Her latest story, "Kept Woman" appeared in January 2021 in the online journal, *Trembling with Fear* (https://horrortree.com/trembling-with-fear-01-31-21/#more-571957).

Doris (Dee) Matthews was raised on a small family farm in central Massachusetts. Her poems have appeared in *Avocet, a Journal of Nature Poetry*, *Cider Press Review*, and the *Worcester Review* along with *Little Red Tree International Poetry Anthology* and *Mother Nature's Trails*. Several of her poems have been nominated and/or selected for Honorable Mention in contests and competitions including *Writer's Digest*. Her chapbook, *Souvenirs* was a finalist in the Kentucky Women Writers' New Voices Competition and was published by Finishing Line Press. Dee is a member of the Worcester County Poetry Association. She retired in 2019 after 41 years of teaching Physical Education to public school children. She enjoys kayaking, hiking, gardening, reading, writing and roaming the fields and woods surrounding her home gathering inspiration and finding serenity.

Jamie McDonough, sometimes called James, lives in a group residence that supports him and assists him with managing his disabilities. He also has a great family that he sees every week. Jamie's many interests include: reading, writing stories and poetry, and watching movies in the theater. At home, he loves cooking but also enjoys eating out and drinking iced coffee. Jamie also enjoys using his computer, playing video games, and spending time with his peers, friends and providers. He especially loves sharing his poetry with others.

Lauren Milka is a Massachusetts resident. She enjoys reading and writing fiction in her spare time.

Sue Moreines is a retired child psychologist who now has time to focus on writing about struggles and overcoming adversity. Always seeking to pay-it-forward, Sue and her rescue dog Daisy volunteer at the library to allow young children the opportunity to practice reading, improve their skills and enjoy the benefits of pet therapy.

Aidan Needle graduated from Athol high school in 2021. Aidan plans to study poetry and writing at a liberal arts college hidden behind thickets and vines. He/they have been published in Quabbin Quills' past anthology *Voices of the Valley* and was the first annual winner of the Quabbin Quills Scholarship which Aidan encourages all students to participate! One day, Aidan would like to live in a small home at the edge of Yosemite and read and write all day. Aidan uses he/they pronouns.

Christine Noyes has spent her life re-inventing herself, becoming an accomplished chef, a sales representative, an entrepreneur, and now a writer and illustrator. She moved to Orange, Massachusetts with her husband Al where, after Al's passing, Chris remains today.

Chris is the author and illustrator of the Big Al Children's Books - *A Big Al Bear Hug, Big Al Helps Clean the Park, The Case of the Missing Cooler, Big Al's Treasure*, and a *Big Al Coloring Book*—all inspired by her late husband. She has also published a memoir, *Close Enough to Perfect*, and her novel *A Picture of Pretense* is due to be released in 2021. When not at her keyboard, she can be found in her kitchen: back to her roots and love of cooking.

For more info, go to: www.BearHugBooks.net
and www.CloseEnoughtoPerfect.com

Kathleen A Rogers is a retired reading specialist who lives in Attleboro, Massachusetts. Writing has always been a part of my life. She has written many books (unpublished) for the classroom and for her grandchildren. Last year, she self-published her first adult novel, *The Loss Of You* and a second novel is nearly finished.

Shonna Ryan resides in New Bedford, MA with her husband, son, and tuxedo cats. When she isn't working, hiking, or playing football, she is writing horror short stories or chipping away at her decade long work-in-progress, a post-apocalyptic sci-fi trilogy. To read more from Shonna, visit her blog: http://murderousintelligent.blogspot.com/

Gerard Sarnat won San Francisco Poetry's 2020 Contest, the Poetry in the Arts First Place Award plus the Dorfman Prize, and has been nominated for handfuls of 2021 and previous Pushcarts, plus Best of the Net Awards. Gerry is widely published in *The North Meridian Review, Buddhist Poetry Review, Gargoyle, Main Street Rag, New Delta Review, Northampton Review, New Haven Poetry Institute, Texas Review, Vonnegut Journal, Brooklyn Review, San Francisco Magazine, Monterey Poetry Review, The Los Angeles Review, New York Times, London Reader* and *Review Berlin* as well as by Harvard, Stanford, Dartmouth, Penn, Chicago and Columbia presses. He has authored the collections *Homeless Chronicles* (2010), *Disputes* (2012), *17s* (2014), *Melting the Ice King* (2016). Gerry is a physician who has built and staffed clinics for the marginalized as well as a Stanford professor and healthcare CEO. Currently he is devoting energy/resources to deal with climate justice, and serves on Climate Action Now's board. Gerry's been married since 1969 with three kids plus six grandsons, and is looking forward to future granddaughters. Thanks to Quabbin Quills for a gander. Happy odd new year, Gerry. For more info go to: gerardsarnat.com

Nancy Barker Sawyer lives in Shirley, MA and has raised two sons, has two grandchildren, and one great grandson. She won the Amherst Society Poetic Achievement Award and is included in *American Poetry Annual* for her poem "Voices." She has also been published in *Great Britain's Poetry Today* for her work entitled "Memory." Nancy is quite involved with Community Theater and has found a new passion for working as a film extra in addition to her work as a clinician in a mental health agency.

Harvey Silverman is a retired physician who writes nonfiction primarily for his own enjoyment. His nonfiction stories have appeared in *Queen's Quarterly, Avalon Literary Review, Ocotillo Review*, and elsewhere.

Chele Shell Pedersen Smith is a contemporary author smitten with romance, comedy, mystery, spirituality, and speculative what-ifs. Writing since sixth grade, she finally began following her dreams as she hit the big 5-0; first as a published author in 2017, and then graduating from Mount Wachusett Community College in 2019 with a degree in professional writing, where she won the Excellence in Writing award. In 2019, she also achieved another long-time writing dream when her story was accepted in *Guideposts Magazine!* Currently, Chele lives in Ashburnham, Massachusetts and is the author of five novels; *Behind Frenemy Lines, The Pearly Gates Phone Company, Chronicle of the Century, The Mysterious Gifts of Tinsel Town,* and *The Epochracy Files,* which features a different and fuller version of Gas Station Time Machine. When she's not daydreaming about dialogues or quirky realms, Chele is a pharmacy technician and college writing tutor who thinks any day is Taco Tuesday.

Lorri Ventura is a retired special education administrator living in Massachusetts. Her poems have been featured in several anthologies.

Jessica Vincent is a proud New England native with a small farm in rural western Massachusetts. Branching out from poetry and short stories, Jessica published a children's book entitled *A Gnome in My Home.* She has a deep appreciation for the extremes of childhood joviality and somber contemplation.

Dr. Thomas Reed Willemain is an emeritus professor of statistics, software entrepreneur, and former intelligence officer. He holds degrees from Princeton University and Massachusetts Institute of Technology. His flash fiction has appeared in *Burningword Literary Journal, Hobart, Detritus Online, The Medley, Drunk Monkeys,* and *Tamarind.* His memoir, *Working on the Dark Side of the Moon: Life Inside the National Security Agency* was published in 2017. A native of South Hadley, Massachusetts, he lives near the Mohawk River in upstate New York. Visit his website: www.TomWillemain.com.

Beyond The Pathway is brought to you by...

...the generous support of the following sponsors.

CHILDREN'S BOOK BY LOCAL AUTHORS

HORATIO MORTIMER LOVED MUSIC
By Sharon A. Harmon
Illustrated By
Siiri Paton

THE LITTLE PINE TREE
By Clare Green

Illustrated By
Zackery Zdinak

WHOSE CAT IS THAT?
By Phyllis Cochran

Illustrated By
Jackie Peoples

DON GATEAU THE THREE-LEGGED CAT OF SEBORGA
By Diane Kane

Illustrated By
Linda McCluskey

NOWEY DISCOVERS
By Marsha LaCroix

Illustrated
By J LaCroix

ALSO, AVALAILABE IN LOCAL STORES: BATES CRAFTERS-
THE KITCHEN GARDEN-PETERSHAM COUNTRY STORE

www.ingramcontent.com/pod-product-compliance
Lightning Source LLC
Chambersburg PA
CBHW070050030726
47506CB00002B/417